PRINCIPALS
and Other Schoolyard Bullies

Short Stories

Nick Fonda

PRINCIPALS
and Other Schoolyard Bullies

Short Stories

Baraka
Books

Montréal

Library and Archives Canada Cataloguing in Publication

Fonda, Nick, 1949-

Principals and other schoolyard bullies: short stories / Nick Fonda.

ISBN 978-1-926824-07-9

I. Title.

PS8611.O547P75 2011   C813'.6   C2011-904814-0

Canada Council   Conseil des Arts
for the Arts   du Canada

We acknowledge the support of the Canada Council for the Arts which last year invested $20.1 million in writing and publishing throughout Canada.

Cover by Folio infographie
Cover illustration by Denis Palmer
Illustrations by Denis Palmer
Book design by Folio infographie

Legal Deposit, 3rd quarter, 2011
Bibliothèque et Archives nationales du Québec
Library and Archives Canada

Published by Baraka Books of Montreal
6977, rue Lacroix
Montréal, Québec H4E 2V4
Telephone: 514 808-8504
info@barakabooks.com
www.barakabooks.com

Printed and bound in Quebec

Trade Distribution & Returns
Canada:
LitDistCo
1-800-591-6250; orders@litdistco.ca

United States:
Independent Publishers Group
1-800-888-4741 (IPG1)

Contents

The Last Day of School

"Are you nervous?"

"No," said Adrian, "I don't think so."

"Well then," asked his aunt, "are you excited?"

"Um, yes, maybe a little," he replied. Then a moment later he added, "Curious. I think most of all, I'm curious."

"Humm," said his aunt. "You're a thoughtful one, aren't you? What do you imagine it's going to be like?"

"I don't know," said Adrian. "I really don't know. It should be ok, though. It should be interesting. It'll be different. I like trying new things."

"Yes, I think you do," mused his aunt. Then, despite herself, she asked, "Tell me, after two weeks with us, how do you like it?"

"I like it," said Adrian and it wasn't the words that reassured his aunt so much as the way he delivered them, quickly, without hesitation, without reserve.

"Good," she said. "I'm glad. We were a little worried, you know. Not worried perhaps, but apprehensive."

"Doesn't that mean the same thing?" Adrian asked.

"I guess it does," his aunt smiled. "Maybe I should have said we were a little uncertain."

"Why?" Adrian asked.

"Well," his aunt gave a little laugh. "Neither your uncle nor I have ever had any experience with children. I think maybe I babysat once when I was a teenager. When your mom called me to ask if you could stay with us I said yes right away, but the moment she hung up, I remember, I turned to Gord and said, 'What have I done?!' Don't get me wrong, Adrian. Gord and I have always loved you. You were an adorable child and you're growing into a fine young man, but it's one thing to see your nephew a few times a year and a very different thing to have him living with you. And I want you to know it's been nice for us."

"Me too," said Adrian. "I'm enjoying it."

"Oh! Look at that. I almost drove right by," exclaimed his aunt, turning the small car into the school parking lot, which was already starting to fill. "Here, I think I can take this spot. I shouldn't be very long."

Adrian's aunt swung the vehicle deftly into a vacant spot, turned off the ignition, reached to the back seat for her handbag and then, just as she reached for the door handle, she stopped and turned back towards her nephew.

"Adrian, what I mentioned earlier? If it doesn't work out, for any reason, tell us right away. Even if it's something small. Ok?"

"Ok."

"Promise?"

"I promise. But it should work out. School should be ok."

"Good. Let's go."

Adrian climbed out of the car and followed his aunt across a few yards of pavement to a set of double doors. His aunt tried one and then the other. Both were locked. She tried knocking and then, with her hand shading her eyes, she put her head close to the glass to try to see into the building.

"That's annoying," Adrian's aunt said. "They asked us to be here by 8:15 and it's almost that now."

"Maybe there's another door," said Adrian. "Want me to go look?"

Even as they turned away from the doors, a small, yellow car sputtered into the parking lot. A moment later, a young woman with a blonde pony tail jumped out, her arms full of binders and books, and greeted them with a big smile.

"The door's locked, eh?" she called to them. "I've got a key."

A key ring with half a dozen keys and a small silver cat hung suspended from the baby finger of her left hand.

"Would you mind opening for me?" she asked. "It's the square key."

It was Adrian who reached out and took the key ring and, a few seconds later, pulled open the door to let his aunt and the lady with the blonde pony tail in.

"Thanks," she said as he slid the key ring back onto her extended pinkie finger. "Are you a new student by any chance?"

"Yes," said Adrian.

"We're here to see the principal, Mr. Walters," said Adrian's aunt. "We're supposed to meet him at 8:15. Where would his office be?"

"On the second floor. Follow me up. I'll show you where it is. I'm Miss Blenheim, by the way."

"This is Adrian and I'm Roberta Simon, Adrian's aunt. Pleased to meet you."

"Like Blenheim Castle?" Adrian asked.

"Why, yes!" laughed Miss Blenheim. "Just like Blenheim Castle. You're the first person outside of my own family I've ever met who knew about Blenheim Castle. How do you know about it?"

"I'm not sure," said Adrian. "Winston Churchill, I guess. We had a dog named Winston Churchill and I read up on him. On the real Winston Churchill, I mean."

"I bet you had a bulldog," said Miss Blenheim.

"Yes!" said Adrian who couldn't help smiling. "How did you know?"

"Lucky guess," said Miss Blenheim, smiling back. "That's Mr. Walter's office, right here. He should be along soon."

"Thank you," said Adrian's aunt. "It was nice meeting you."

"Nice meeting you too," replied Miss Blenheim. "What grade are you in Adrian?"

"I don't know."

"Adrian's been homeschooled by his parents," his aunt explained. "This is going to be his first experience with formal schooling."

"Well!" said Miss Blenheim. "I hope it goes well. You might even be in my class. You're not eleven by any chance, are you?"

"I'm ten," said Adrian.

"Maybe I'll have you in my class next year. Good luck."

Miss Blenheim ducked into a doorway a few steps away and smiled at them a few minutes later when she re-emerged. They watched her walk to the end of the hall and begin climbing another flight of stairs.

Over the next ten minutes, several other people passed by. Some nodded hello and others ignored them completely. At a certain point, a woman who turned out to be the school secretary arrived and unlocked the door outside which they were standing and informed them that Mr. Walters would be along any minute. She poked her head out a moment later to offer Adrian's aunt a cup of coffee.

"Thanks, no," she said. "I've had my cup for the day."

Still they waited. Adrian and his aunt walked a few paces up the corridor and then a few paces down, eventually walking the whole length of the corridor. They stopped in front of the four different bulletin boards, each one displaying what must have been students' work.

Eventually, Adrian noticed a man coming up the hallway. He walked slowly and deliberately, as if he had all the time in the world to get to his destination. He was neither tall nor short but carried a certain bulk on his frame. He walked with his feet splayed out, almost as if he were walking with flippers on his feet. As he came closer, Adrian noticed that a rather bushy moustache drooped over his mouth and a large pair of glasses sat on the bridge of his nose.

"Mr. Walters?" asked his aunt, as he approached them.

"Yes," he replied with little enthusiasm.

"Good morning. I'm Roberta Simon. I spoke to you yesterday about enrolling my nephew Adrian."

"Right," said Mr. Walters, glancing quickly at Adrian and then looking away just as quickly. "I'll be with you in a minute."

He strolled into his office leaving Adrian and his aunt standing in the hallway. Adrian's aunt looked down at him, her eyebrows raised in a look of silent surprise and shrugged her shoulders.

Adrian was about to ask his aunt if she thought that Mr. Walters didn't look like a sleepy walrus, but he caught himself and remained silent.

It was a long, few minutes before the secretary came out and invited Adrian and his aunt into the principal's office. They entered what was clearly the secretary's office and then through an open door to the left into that of the principal. Mr. Walters was seated at his desk, half turned towards a computer monitor. He didn't get up as they came in.

"Have a seat," he said, his eyes focussed on the screen, his fingers on the keyboard.

"Thank you," said his aunt.

Adrian let his bookbag slide to the floor and sat on one of the two well-padded chairs that were just a little too big for him. He looked at Mr. Walters sitting in three quarters profile, hardly more than an arm's length or two across a bare expanse of desk. He had a very round head, all the rounder for being sparsely covered in wispy grey-brown hair. There was a pudginess to his neck and jaws, accentuated by deep folds. His skin looked raw and red, like tough weather-beaten leather. Up close, thought Adrian, he looked even more like a walrus.

"So, you want to register your son in our school," he said, still looking at the screen.

"My nephew. Adrian's parents are out of the country for an extended period. I'm his maternal aunt. Adrian's going to be living with us until they return."

"Humm. It's too bad you didn't register him last week. Our budget allocation is set according to our enrolment on the fifteenth."

Adrian wasn't at all sure what Mr. Walters was talking about and he turned towards his aunt. He sensed that she too was puzzled.

"Now, what school is he transferring from?" continued Mr. Walters, his eyes still on the monitor.

"He's not transferring from any school," Adrian's aunt said. "So far, Adrian's been homeschooled."

"Homeschooled?" For the first time since they'd come into the office, Mr. Walters looked at them. He pushed his glasses up on the bridge of his nose and blinked his eyes. His voice had risen as he asked his question and now he looked at Adrian and his aunt with undisguised suspicion.

After a long moment of silence, Adrian's aunt, in a voice that seemed to be struggling to stay calm and even, said, "Yes, he was homeschooled."

There was another moment of silence. Finally Mr. Walters spoke, "Parents do a great disservice to their children when they homeschool. They're not professionals. Communicating knowledge is a job for professionals. And homeschooled children never acquire the social skills they need to function properly."

As the principal spoke, Adrian could sense his aunt growing tense. He turned his eyes towards her and saw that she was sitting almost at the edge of her chair, her back ramrod straight, her chin thrust forward, her face slightly flushed. When she spoke, her voice had a crispness that Adrian had never heard before.

"Is it possible to enroll Adrian in this school?"

"Oh, yes, of course. All the schools in this Board are inclusive and welcoming. The welfare of our students is our number one priority," said Mr. Walrus, turning back to his monitor.

There were a few more minutes of questions, which seemed to be addressed more to the screen than to Adrian or his aunt. Then, for the second time, the principal turned towards the two of them.

"I'm going to try him in Grade 5, just because of his age. He's probably going to be quite a bit behind the others, but it might be hard for him to adjust socially in a Grade 4 group. All our students use laptops and that will be something else for him to learn. We'll get him one in a few days. You'll have to sign for it. For today, we can probably find him a spare."

He turned from them again, pressed a button on his phone and called, "Miss Thibault, could you show these people up to Ms Camlet's class?"

❧

"Where am I going to put him?" were the first words that Adrian heard Ms Camlet speak.

"I know," replied Miss Thibault sympathetically. "But the other Grade 5 has thirty-two in it and you only had twenty-nine."

"Yes! But look at the class I've got!"

"I'm sorry," said Miss Thibault with a shrug of her shoulders.

"Anyway. I'll look after him."

Adrian and his aunt were shown the locker he would be sharing with another student and the table at which he would be sitting, with three others. For today, Miss Camlet informed him, he would take the seat of a boy named Ralph whom she expected to be absent. When his aunt left, she bent to give him a kiss on the cheek and a hug. She kept her hands on his shoulders for an extra few seconds and looked into his eyes, as if she were searching for something.

"Will you be alright?" she asked.

"Sure," said Adrian, although as he watched her walk down the hallway, he felt some of his certainty leaving with her.

"I'm on bus duty this morning," Ms Camlet informed him, "so you better come down with me. I'll show you where your class lines up. Your class is 5 C. You'll see that painted on the pavement. That's where you'll line up with your class every time you come in: first thing in the morning, after the morning recess and after the lunch hour recess. Do you understand? You've got a few minutes to play right now before the bell rings."

Adrian stood alone and surveyed the space before him, which only half an hour ago had been totally empty and was now overflowing with children. Some were walking slowly from the area where the yellow school buses were disgorging them, near where his aunt had earlier parked her car, but most were standing in small groups on a surprisingly vast expanse of pavement. A smaller number could be found on a much larger green area given over to a baseball diamond and soccer field which could be reached by going up a very small bank.

When the bell rang, a few minutes later, Adrian turned from where he stood to walk the few paces to the spot Ms Camlet had told him his class was to line up. He was surprised that half a dozen girls were already in line. Even as he started walking he found the space filled with other bodies and it took him a couple of seconds to realize that he was moving perpendicular to the fast-forming lines. It took him a minute but he made it to the 5 C line and placed himself behind a short girl whose brown hair was streaked with an unnaturally bright shade of red.

Adrian wondered if he'd been staring at her because she spun towards him, fixed him with angry, glaring eyes and said, "This isn't your line. This is 5 C."

"I'm in 5 C," he replied.

She stared at him for a minute then she hissed, "Creep," and turned to face the school.

A half second later Adrian was thrown forward into the red-streaked girl by someone who had smashed into his back.

"Ow!" he called out and then, realizing he had caused a chain reaction, he quickly said, "Sorry. I'm sorry. Someone pushed me."

There were hoots and catcalls from behind him while those in front of him called him a jerk, a twit, a nerd and other names he tried not to hear. Almost at the same time that he had righted himself, wondering if there was going to be a bruise on his back, Ms Camlet was standing beside him.

"Don't cause trouble your first day," she threatened, "You'll regret it if you do. Understand?"

Adrian looked up at her, puzzled and perplexed and completely unsure what to do or what to say. He remained silent. She glared at him for a couple of seconds and then turned her attention elsewhere as one line after the other filed into the school, the 5 C group going last.

Adrian, taking his cue from the others, went to his locker, and after enduring an elbow to his ribs, which may or may not have been accidental, hung up his light jacket, and retrieved from his book bag a scribbler and a pencil case, both new. He followed his locker mate—a dark-haired, taciturn boy who had neither greeted Adrian, nor returned his greeting—at a safe distance into the classroom and seated himself at the table Ms Camlet had earlier assigned him.

The next ten or twelve minutes were a confusing cacophony of scraping chairs, laughter, snippets of conversation and dropped objects. Adrian sat silent, feeling ever more isolated and alone. A bell rang, startling him, and a moment later Ms Camlet, after two or three attempts, brought silence to the room.

"We have a new student with us, class, and I'd like you all to meet him," she announced. "Adrian, could you stand and introduce yourself."

Caught unaware, Adrian felt suddenly and unaccustomedly shy. He stood and looked at the faces around him, at eyes which seemed to be largely filled with indifference, although he also saw what might have been hostility.

"My name is Adrian Bretarski," he began and stopped short, uncertain what else he might be expected to say.

"Adrian the Retard!" a voice called out, supported by a wave of giggles and snickering that Ms Camlet's stern voice cut short.

"Can you tell us a little about yourself, Adrian," said Ms Camlet, trying bravely to salvage the moment. "What school were you in before coming here?" she continued, offering as safe and innocuous a question as she could imagine. She was surprised that her new pupil hesitated as he did before replying and even more surprised—a surprise mixed with outrage—at the short but brutish burst of laughter that came from one corner of the classroom.

Without his teacher's prompting or permission, Adrian sat down after that, feeling as much hurt as confused. It was several minutes before he raised his head again, and quite some time after that before he began to steal glances around the room to try to make sense of this strange new world in which he found himself.

When the recess bell rang, releasing the class into the hallway and onto the playground, he hung back, studiously watchful and a little wary. He was conscious of the fact that in some way or other he didn't fit in with those around him, but he couldn't understand why. Yet, he was not without the instinct that made him wish to belong. Standing alone, he observed, trying to decide whom he might try to approach, and how best to do it. But by the time he had selected a pair of boys in his class who seemed, if not perfectly safe at least noticeably less dangerous, the bell rang and it was time to form a single file.

Mindful of what had happened earlier that morning he took his time lining up and kept well away from the girl with red-streaked hair. He also took note of who was behind him. He filed in dutifully with the others and reached his locker feeling a sense of accomplishment, for the shove or push he had anticipated had not come.

But when he opened his locker, his heart fell. His school bag, which had been zipped shut, was open, as was his lunch bag, and the food his aunt had prepared was spilled on the locker floor. He looked around, half expecting to see someone smirking at him, but there was no one looking at him, nor paying the least attention.

Adrian's food had been carefully wrapped and packaged, so even though it had been spilled, he had been able to eat everything. Yet, lunch in the cafeteria had been far from pleasant. The cafeteria was impossibly noisy and crowded. He had found a place to squeeze himself in, but neither of the two people beside him, nor the few sitting across from him, seemed interested in speaking to him. Worse, twice he was hit by someone passing behind him. The first time he got a knee in the small of his back. The second time, someone clipped him behind the ear with the hard plastic corner of a cafeteria tray. It was a sharp, crisp blow and, even though Adrian managed to stifle the cry which came unbidden to his lips, he could not prevent his eyes from momentarily tearing up.

The two boys whom Adrian had thought of approaching at recess were nowhere to be seen after lunch. He found himself being stared at by the boy who had hit him with the cafeteria tray, one of the group of boys in his class who had laughed at him in the morning. Adrian drifted away, determined to search out someone with whom he might try to strike up a conversation, if not a friendship. He was looking for someone else who seemed alone, or for a small group of two or three.

When they lined up to go in after lunch, he was again jostled from behind by unseen hands.

Then, towards the end of the afternoon, when the class was supposedly doing an art activity and there was a certain amount of coming and going, Adrian found himself at the wrong end of a pencil.

He was concentrated on his artwork, feeling pleased for the first time that day because two of his classmates, walking by, had glanced at his work and spoken to him, to say his drawing was nice. Ms Camlet had also come by and had fussed a little over his work, telling him he had a talent for art. Then, sensing someone else over his shoulder, he had looked up to find Steven, the boy with the tray, standing over him.

"Is that supposed to be a donkey or an ass?"

"What?"

"That!" And Steven bent forward towards the paper on Adrian's desk and with a quick, violent motion, slashed a dark line across the drawing, tearing the paper.

"Hey!" Adrian jumped to his feet to confront the bigger boy, knocking over his chair.

"Why'd you do that?"

"What's going on?" Ms Camlet was making her way quickly across the room.

"It was an accident, Retard."

The words, so blatantly false, the tone, the mocking smirk, the tension which had been building all day caused something to boil over, and Adrian, with an anger he'd never before experienced, pushed the class bully.

Steven, who was big and strong and quick, who had been in lots of schoolyard fights, and who had prepared for this conflict with the tactical precision of a chess master, swung back, still holding his pencil, and as the sharp, graphite tip slashed Adrian's cheek, it broke and remained deep in the soft flesh.

Ms Camlet was there, no more than a second or two too late. Frustrated and angry, but also impotent in the face of Steven's protests of innocence, "It was an accident. He pushed me first," she put a protective arm around Adrian, and brought him quickly to the classroom door.

"I know it hurts," she said to Adrian, "but it's not bleeding very much and you'll be ok. I'll have someone bring you down to Miss Thibault and she'll patch you up. And Adrian? I know it's been a hard day for you, but tomorrow will be better. Thing's will go well tomorrow."

"Alison," she called, "bring Adrian down to see Miss Thibault, will you please?"

The Sour Taste of Revenge

I recognized him right away. He limped in and I knew, instantly and with absolute certainty, it was Billy, even though I hadn't seen him in almost twenty years.

He didn't look very good, but that is true of many of the people who come through the doors and to my reception desk. It's especially true at night, and it was only half an hour before the end of my shift when he came in. He was noticeably favouring his right leg and his left arm was crossed over his chest. His right hand was supporting his left elbow. My first guess was a broken collar bone. To look at his face, I guessed that he'd been in a fight. The skin was blotchy. There was dried blood and noticeable swelling near his left eye. He was alone.

I watched him painfully take the dozen steps that separate the entrance from the desk. He had the same dark, wavy hair he'd had as a child, and the olive skin. He hadn't grown to more than average height and he was slim. He had one of those tough, wiry bodies. As I watched him it came to me that he had his mother's build. He moved with his shoulders slumped forward, keeping his head half down. He raised it twice, once to locate the desk and again to check that he was moving towards it. His dark eyes were half-hooded, as if his eyelids were too heavy to fully open.

His chin was small and his mouth was the same thin, straight, mean gash I remembered.

When he was just a step or two away from me, I turned away from him and back to the screen on my desk. I pretended to be unaware of his presence.

"I have to see a doctor," was the first thing he said. I continued typing on my keyboard and studied my screen for a long minute before turning to him.

"I'll need your health card," I replied, "and, if you've been here before, your clinic card as well. It's burgundy in colour." I looked straight at him as I spoke, challenging his eyes to recognize who I was. Perhaps under different circumstances, he might have. Pain can short-circuit a lot of the brain's activity.

"You can sit down if you want," I added, pointing to the chair beside him. This wasn't politeness or concern. I said it knowing that any change in position would bring with it a fresh wave of pain.

He looked at the chair for a long minute but stayed standing. He released his grip on his left elbow and reached slowly and gingerly towards his back pocket. He had to shift his shoulders and when he did his face twisted with pain. His right hand went quickly back to his left elbow and he took in a gasp of air. His eyes came up to meet mine. Behind the half-hooded lids, they were red-rimmed and bloodshot, brimming with supplication.

"It's in my back pocket. I can't reach it."

"I need your health card and your clinic card, if you have one," I repeated, as if I hadn't heard a word he had said. I was surprised at how easy it was to ignore the begging note in his voice, the pleading in his dark eyes. Still, I didn't trust myself. I turned back to my screen. I gave myself the task of verifying a schedule I'd looked at only minutes before.

❦

We were living in the middle of three apartments which had been carved out of an old wood-frame house on Laurier Street. Looking back, I think the apartment was probably a real dump. Laurier Street, like most of the neighbourhood that used to be known as Cartierville, has been extensively gentrified. But twenty years ago, the north end of the street especially, was on the wrong side of the proverbial tracks. The house itself is no longer there. It was torn down at some point and replaced by an attractive eight-unit apartment block. Much of the yard we played in—and where this all happened—is now parking spaces or someone's kitchen. Ironically, I think it was the large, fenced-in yard that had decided my parents to take the apartment.

Upstairs from us lived a nice old man we knew as Mr. Argent. He was almost always home, but we never heard him. In the summer, we might see him on his balcony, working away at something. We'd been told that he was an artist of some kind but we never saw him drawing or painting. He always smiled and waved at us if we called hello, then he'd turn back to his work. I think children made him shy. He never gave out candy at Hallowe'en. He kept his door shut and his lights off to discourage any trick or treaters. But he'd come downstairs, well before dark, and give us homemade cookies. "There's no sugar in these," he'd tell us, his voice implying they were especially good because of this. We, as children, didn't share his enthusiasm for sugar-free foods and we would leave them in a drawer to petrify. Mr. Argent had lived upstairs long before we moved in, and as far as I know, continued to live there long after we left.

Downstairs was different. In the three years we lived on Laurier Street, there were always new tenants in the downstairs apartment, the last of whom was Billy; that is, Billy and his parents were the last tenants we knew. It was because of Billy or, more accurately, because of Billy's parents, that we left.

Almost from the moment I met Billy, I disliked and feared him.

We'd watched the previous neighbours move out and, when a truck appeared later the same day bringing the new tenants, I was excited to see that they had a child, a boy, who seemed to be about our age. I would have preferred a girl, but a boy was better than nothing. I would have, I thought, someone other than just my brother, Marhan, to play with. I dragged Marhan outside with me and we parked ourselves noticeably in the middle of the yard and kicked our old soccer ball back and forth. It was the longest time before our new neighbour came outside.

At first, I thought he might be like us because, under his black hair, his face seemed dark. He was a little bigger than Marhan, but he was smaller than me. He crossed part of the way towards us, but when I said hi to him he stopped and turned his back to us. I ignored him for a minute and when he looked at us again I tried a second time. This time, he stared at us in silence, his head slightly lowered so that he glowered from under his scowling eyebrows. I felt disappointed. This wasn't going to be a new friend to play with. I turned back to Marhan, but I had lost much of my enthusiasm for kicking our old soccer ball.

A moment later, Marhan's errant kick sent the ball into the space between me and the new boy. I ran towards the ball to kick it back. All of a sudden, the new boy was in front of me, slamming into me and knocking me to the ground. He grabbed the ball in both hands, turned and ran towards the back fence. I remained on the ground for a minute, probably more surprised than hurt, but in tears just the same. Then Marhan was running by me, following the new boy, yelling for the ball. The new boy stopped, looked at Marhan, then kicked the ball, not back to Marhan, but away from us, over the fence that separated the large back yard from the ravine that led down to the brook below.

"That's our ball!"

"Why'd you do that?"

"How are we going to get it back?"

The new boy said nothing. He stared at us with a smile I had never seen before, a smile of smug self-satisfaction, of defiance and challenge. He was immensely pleased with what he had done. We stared at him, beyond words, puzzled and confused.

The next moment his mother was at her back door. She had short dark hair and angular features. She was very thin and her shoulders were slightly stooped. She had a cigarette in one hand and a candy bar in the other.

"Come here, Billy," she called.

Billy turned his head to look at her but he didn't move.

"Billy, come here!" she called again in a voice that was already noticeably more strident.

Billy continued to stare at her, his head slightly lowered, his mouth set in a thin line. Marhan and I stood, probably with our mouths hanging open. If kicking the ball into the ravine had surprised us, what we were watching now was beyond the scope of our imaginations.

"Come here!" she yelled again, the anger now unmistakable in her voice. Then, a fraction of a second later, her voice changed completely. It became gently and cloyingly sweet. "Look, Billy! Look what Mommy has for her sweet, little boy. Come and get it."

Billy stood still for a fraction of a second longer but we could see him wavering as his mother waved the chocolate bar in the air. Without so much as a glance at us, Billy ran to his mother.

"You're a good boy, Billy," she said to him. "Mommy wants you to stay away from those bad children." She said this, raising her eyes and looking at us. She didn't so much give Billy the chocolate bar as he grabbed it from her hand. She ushered Billy through the door. Billy was totally absorbed in ripping the wrapper off the bar with short, violent movements. Billy's mom continued glaring at us over her shoulder until the door slammed shut behind her.

I don't remember how we got our ball back, or even if we did. I do remember that our subsequent encounters with Billy were no more pleasant than the first. He was a greedy, aggressive, spiteful child who, despite his size, was a terror both in the neighbourhood and on the school playground. Marhan and I did our best to keep our distance.

The incident occurred not many months after Billy arrived. It was summer when he moved in. The day we moved out was cold and damp and the maple in the yard had lost the last of its leaves.

A week or two before the incident, our maternal grandfather, our Panpan, had come to stay with us. He had last seen me as an infant and he had never seen Marhan. I was now eight and Marhan five. Panpan was a small, stooped man with white hair and strange-looking, wire-framed glasses. His English was heavily accented and communication wasn't easy for us because, even though our parents still spoke Khasi between themselves, English had become the lingua franca of our household.

It was a Saturday evening. For the first time since they'd become parents, our mother and father were going out together, unencumbered by offspring. Unlike most children, we had never had a babysitter. Either our dad or our mom was always at home with us. It was the arrival of Panpan that had created this opportunity for them to have a child-free evening.

It was dusk, the end of a warm fall day. Marhan and I had gone outside after supper, determined to ignore the rapidly cooling air and the fading light because the longer we managed to stay outside the longer we would defer our bedtime. We had bargained with Panpan to stay out as long as there was light. For a while he had also been outside, on the balcony, reading, until he had called to us, "A few more minutes, yes?"

Marhan and I had been on the verge of going in when we heard a car arrive. We stayed behind the maple tree, listening. We heard a car door slam shut, then a second and a third. We heard Billy's mom calling him and, a long moment later, their apartment door slamming shut.

Pleased to have squeezed the last bit of lingering light out of the sky, and relieved that the coast was clear, we rose to cross the yard and go into the house. We hadn't taken more than ten steps when Billy suddenly appeared in front of us. I think I might have gasped or screamed. I know, because this is such a visceral memory, I know that my stomach knotted up, that I felt fear, that I felt a premonition that something bad was about to happen.

"I want to play," he said to us. "Do you want to play?"

"No," said Marhan.

"We have to go in," I said, older, desperate to sound authoritative.

"Why don't you play? I want to play."

"No."

"We have to go in."

"Come on. You can play with me."

"I don't want to play with you."

"We have to go in. Come along, Marhan."

I brushed by my brother to the left so that Marhan was between Billy and me. I tried to keep my head up. As I went by Marhan, I took his left hand to pull him along.

"Play with me!" Billy screamed, his voice angry.

I pressed ahead, pulling on Marhan. Suddenly, Marhan cried out and my right arm was straight out behind me. Billy had grabbed Marhan's other arm. He was holding it with both hands and pulling. His face was an angry, hateful, spiteful grimace.

"I want to play!" he screamed at me.

"Oww! Let go!"

"Let my brother go!"

Marhan and I were both screaming. Stupidly, I held on to Marhan for a long few seconds, not knowing what else to do.

When I let go, Billy fell backwards and Marhan on top of him. I didn't stop to look. I let go and turned to run for Panpan. Amazingly, he was there, two steps away.

Then he was past me and when I turned he was bent over, pulling Billy off Marhan. Billy's arms never seemed to stop swinging the whole time and, as Panpan pulled Billy away, Panpan's wire-framed glasses flew off his face and onto the lawn.

As quickly as that, it was all over. Billy ran off, but as he ran by me, he spit at me and pushed me so that I fell down. Marhan, undaunted and unblemished, came off the ground as if nothing had ever happened. I was the one who burst into tears. Panpan found his glasses and with an arm around each of us walked us back to the house, trying to make us laugh. It wasn't until we got inside that I saw that my grandfather had been cut and that there was a thin line of dark blood along the edge of his cheekbone.

That was Saturday. It was six days later, on a Friday afternoon, that two policemen rang the bell. They were big and seemed to fill up the kitchen door. They wore black boots with thick, heavy soles. They carried guns in thick, heavy, black holsters so only a bit of the pistol butt showed. They wore dark blue jackets.

They sat at the kitchen table, their dark hats on the table but their jackets on, and spent a long time talking to Panpan. My mother, her face grim, sat with them. Sometimes, she repeated what Panpan said. One of the policemen, his hands folded on the table in front of him, asked Panpan question after question. The other one wrote everything down on paper. Slowly my mother's face relaxed. The policeman who had been writing put down his pad of paper and put his pen into a shirt pocket.

A week after that came a lawyer's letter demanding a huge sum of money for damages.

We moved, less than a month later, to the fourth floor of a block on Simpson Street pretentiously called Golden Towers. The apartment was very nice and everything looked almost new, but it was small. It felt cramped and, of course, there was no yard to play in. We stayed there for the next five years, until my parents bought the house on Garrand Street. It had a lovely yard, but by that time we were no longer children and never played in it.

୧୬

"This it?" he asked holding out a plastic card. He wasn't standing on his own, but leaning onto the reception desk. I could smell him now: stale smoke, alcohol, sweat—a sour, vile smell that made me want to put my hand on my nose and mouth.

The health card is unmistakable with its bright sun shining from the top left corner. The hand holding it out—rough, cracked skin; dirty, broken nails—was unsteady. As I reached for it I looked towards him, searching out his eyes, silently daring him to meet my challenging stare. And if I said to him, "No, this isn't the card," how would those eyes, clouded by alcohol and preoccupied by pain, react?

Or if I brushed my hand against the card and knocked it to the floor, how would the broken collar bone bend to pick it up?

Or if I took the card and, like some practiced card shark, flung it brazenly to the other end of the lobby?

I swiped the card, asked the perfunctory questions, directed the patient to the waiting room where four others sat nursing their own ailments with silent worry. There are nights when triage is difficult. Precedence is given to the more serious cases. A heart attack gets seen before a broken arm. An accident victim goes before an asthma attack.

The last temptation was to place the folder marked William Wendell Webster, twenty-seven year old male with a suspected collarbone fracture and multiple abrasions, on the bottom of the small pile of folders, underneath the false croup, the flu, and the stomach cramps.

In the end, I dropped the folder on top where Dr. Pirano saw it just a few minutes later and called Billy's name.

Judy arrived to start her shift and, at 11 pm, I walked out the door and into the cool night air. I breathed deeply through my nostrils and savoured the faint, crisp, clean breeze. There was no more of the sour smell.

The Other Mulroney

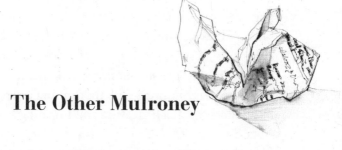

The words infuriated me so much that I snapped the radio off with much more force than necessary; I called the dog, jammed on my outdoor shoes and strode out the door. The air was heavy with humidity and the sky was a low, grey-white cloud, behind which I thought I could make out the sun striving to create some semblance of day. I realized that I should have taken my light jacket, if not my rain gear, but I was fuming inside and in no mood to be reasonable.

In the valley, river fog—like this—sometimes rises thickly off the water in the early dawn. It's a welcome sign for the day that follows will inevitably be warm and sunny.

There's a path that runs up the hill behind the house, through a small woods of birch and beech and maple. The hill is relatively steep in places, with unexpected outcrops of rock emerging from soil soft with centuries of fallen leaves. It runs up the escarpment for what's probably close to a quarter mile and then opens onto a field that Craig Latulippe has left fallow again this year.

The first years I had the dog, I would leash her on this walk, just as surely as when I took her along the road. Lara is part Lab. She's an intelligent animal and fairly well trained; she's not the sort of creature that would mindlessly wander onto a road that sometimes carries too many cars moving too fast. The zoning here is the same as in the village but along this stretch of road everyone is speeding up to, or slowing down from, highway speeds. What I did worry about was a cat sauntering out of a driveway, or a ground hog scurrying leglessly out of a ditch and across the road. It was too easy to imagine Lara running after some small but impossibly quick creature and impaling herself on the front bumper of an innocent car.

In the woods, there was no danger of fatal collisions, but I always worried about a skunk or a porcupine attracting her attention. Now of course, she's old and stays close by, hardly even inclined to bark back at the taunting chatter of red squirrels.

The woods were wet with dew and I was soaked when we stepped into the breeze that was coming off the grassy field. I suddenly felt cold. Again, I wished I'd brought my rain gear, or my jacket.

It was much brighter now that we were out of the woods and the sun was more noticeable, pushing a diffused but promising light across a large patch of sky. Lara made a half-hearted effort to bound into the tall grass, perhaps remembering that when she was young, it was here that I'd unleash her to run free. We turned upriver and walked along the edge of the woods, where we always walked when this field was planted in oats or corn.

The words that had upset me a short while ago came back to me.

"In retrospect, with the benefit of hindsight, Your Honour, I have to agree that I probably should have asked the question."

Were those his exact words? Did a man, bright enough to become Prime Minister, really say that he forgot to ask a question so obvious even a child would know enough to ask?

Is that what had set me off this morning? Was it that wording? Words I imagined my Mulroney saying.

LIKE EVERYONE ELSE ACROSS THE COUNTRY, I have not escaped coverage of the inquiry into our former Prime Minister's business affairs. It was old news that prime ministerial hands had drawn unmarked envelopes stuffed with wads of large denomination bills across a tabletop between coffees and croissants.

Nor could it have been his voice. His voice has always put me on guard. It is the voice of a con man, low-pitched, deep with insincerity, unctuous to the point of being greasy. It was a voice that would lull you to sleep and when you woke you would find your signature on the dotted line.

Maybe it was something else, or perhaps a combination of things. When the realization hit me, I laughed aloud. Lara came back to me, her tail wagging but looking at me as if to say, "Are you ok?" I was ok, even though I was alone and laughing in Craig's empty field. Lara knows I might occasionally talk to myself, or smile to myself when I'm at work, or in the kitchen, but I normally need human company around me to laugh aloud.

"I'm fine. And you're a wonderful dog for asking," I said to Lara. I took her head in my hands and gave her a quick rub behind her ears. She looked up at me, her tongue lolling out of her mouth a little more than usual, her eyes dark and trusting. "Can you still fetch?" I stepped into the woods and found a stick.

❧

I met my Mulroney—Joseph, not Brian—on April 15, 1992. It was easy to imagine my Mulroney standing before a similar board of inquiry. He too would say, with the same arrogant, feigned innocence of his namesake, "In hindsight, I probably should have asked the question."

I can cite the date of our first meeting with accuracy because it was my sixteenth birthday. Sixteen is considered one of those special birthdays, like twenty-one and thirty-five and fifty. For me, it was very special. I was alive and safe, when I could so easily have been dead or worse.

I celebrated the day by enrolling in a new school.

When I woke up that morning, for a long few seconds, I had no idea where I was. As I lay perfectly still, I could tell I was tucked snugly beneath warm bedclothes as if I hadn't moved a muscle all night. My bed was warm and soft and as perfectly comfortable as it was unfamiliar. I was aware of light, of miniscule dust particles drifting idly upwards. It was a broad, soft beam emanating from a crack in the curtains on the wall to my right that gave the room a warm glow. The walls and ceiling I had never before seen and I could make no sense of them. Yet, like the half-light, they seemed welcoming, friendly. The space made me feel I was being cocooned and coddled and cradled. But for a long minute I had no idea where I was. Nor could I guess what time it was.

The where finally came to me. Still, I lay in bed a few minutes more before getting up and going to the window. The floorboards were cold on my bare feet and the glass cold on my fingertips. I looked at my new surroundings under an almost impossibly bright sky: patches of dirty lawn between remaining mounds of sickly snow; mature, deciduous trees a hundred feet away fencing off the neighbour's brick house. The sky was a bright, clear blue punctuated with white, cumulus clouds; a sky my painterly grandmother would teach me to refer to as Coburnesque.

The sun seemed to suggest that it was late, which would make sense. The plane had landed after ten, and there had been customs and almost a three-hour drive after that. I had no memory of actually coming into this house, of putting on the strange pyjamas I wore. There was no sign of my clothes, but there was a blue housecoat hanging on the door.

I found my mother and grandmother already up, my mother like me, barefoot and in pyjamas and housecoat which didn't belong to her.

My grandmother, as she always did, made a fuss over me, talking a mile a minute, asking me questions she never gave me time to answer, hugging me, kissing me, teasing me. And then she was off like a whirlwind to fix me something special for breakfast. My mom said happy birthday and then gave me a hug which seemed to last forever and I realized that she was crying. But I knew they were tears of joy, or rather, tears of relief and gratitude. I wasn't a kid anymore and I knew that my parents had worried more for me than for themselves. The sense of peace I'd felt in the room upstairs still enveloped me and I didn't have any tears to shed, but it felt good to have my mother hug me. I was filled with gratitude to be where I was.

I met Joseph Mulroney towards the end of that same day and my gratitude, at least for a short while, evaporated. What I felt, the first time I saw Joseph Mulroney, was overwhelming fear. If I had seen him in the grey uniform of a Serb border guard, I'd have turned and run, or bowed my head, avoided all eye contact, and hoped that my mother would get me through alive and without too much pain as she had already and so recently done.

I've thought about this a lot over the years, that first reaction.

There was nothing about the man himself that should have set off all my alarm systems flashing danger signs. He was nondescript, like someone who might blandly have stepped out of the pages of a catalogue for men's clothing.

We had been waiting in the hallway for several minutes, staring at unpainted walls made of cinder blocks. There was nothing on the walls other than a few framed montages of smiling graduates from previous years. We had to stand and we were both tired. Eventually, his secretary appeared, led us a few steps down the hall to the next door, and we were in his office. As I followed my mother into the room, in the instant during which I saw Joseph Mulroney, he was in frozen motion behind his desk, bent slightly forward in the act of moving to take his chair. His head was cocked up, so that I saw his eyes staring malevolently up at me from below his eyebrows. His right hand seemed to be reaching back into his jacket pocket, or to his hip, as if for a weapon.

He must have grunted something like, "Come in," and sat down behind his wide desk without shaking my mother's hand, even though she was reaching forward to shake his.

"I understand you're from out of province, or out of country? And you want to enroll your daughter to finish the school year?"

"Yes," said my mother.

"April is a difficult time of the year to move to a new school. It's very close to final exams. Now, before we start, we should make sure that your daughter can be admitted. There are language laws that impose restrictions on who can attend an English school. Were you, or your husband, educated in English in Canada?"

"Yes," said my mother. "We both were."

"Good," he said and turned his eyes on me and asked, "Now, what grade were you in at your last school?"

It took me a second to get my voice and it came out squeaky when I finally said, "I was in Lower 6."

"Suzanne was at Miss Wallace's English School, a small private school in Sarajevo," my mother explained. "It followed the Oxford and Cambridge curriculum. The children sit the O-Level and A-Level exams, as they would if they were attending school in England. Suzanne was preparing to sit five O-Levels, as well as her A-Level in Art."

"I'm not too familiar with that system. We follow the curriculum set by the Ministry in Quebec. I doubt at this point that we could even register Suzanne for the exams. And she couldn't possibly be ready for them. She wouldn't be able to catch up on the whole year's work in six or seven weeks. But we could place her in Grade 11 just to finish the year. Or, we could put her in Grade 10 and it would give her a chance to make friends for next year."

"Oh?" My mother looked over at me and I didn't know what to say.

"I wasn't really thinking of her being in high school next year. She was already looking at maybe starting art school in the fall, if she gets her A-Level. I haven't yet made the arrangements, but I'm sure she can sit her Oxford and Cambridge exams; they can be taken almost anywhere in the world. Right now, I'm trying to get some normalcy back into her life. Suzanne's going to be staying with her grandmother till the end of the school year. I'll be there too, at least for some of the time. I want to get her enrolled in school because she's just sixteen, and right now it would be best for her to be in school."

"Yes, of course," but he didn't sound too convinced. The momentary fear I'd experienced faded and gave way to a certainty that, for a reason I couldn't explain, I was an annoying problem he didn't want to deal with. He wasn't in a position to shoot me or have me thrown into a dungeon, but his attitude towards me wasn't much different; he wanted to be rid of me. "So, in effect, you'd like your daughter to audit classes till the end of the year. Is that correct? She's not going to *Cégep*?"

"No," my mother replied. "At least, at this point, I wouldn't think so. Her brothers did their studies in England and Suzanne was hoping to be accepted into Art School in Edinburgh."

Joseph Mulroney didn't say anything for a moment. He seemed to be thinking something over, trying to reach some sort of decision.

"I'd prefer my daughter be in this school," my mother explained, "I know there's a French high school fifteen or twenty minutes away. And Suzanne could go there. Her French is very adequate. She did three years of elementary school in French in Egypt, and she has spent a summer in France. But she's been doing her schooling in English for the last five years and I think it will be easier for her to continue in English, if possible. Besides, her grandmother now lives just down the road, not even five minutes by car."

"Of course. We'll be glad to have Suzanne here. So, you're good in art? What else are you good in?"

"I don't know," I finally mumbled, and my mother stepped in for me.

"Overall, she's a strong student. Not many girls her age are already sitting an A-level."

"Do you like sports?"

"A little, I guess."

"What sports did you do at your last school?"

"Well, none, really."

"Miss Wallace's was a very small school," my mother explained. "I think there may have been thirty-five or forty

pupils in all. It operated out of an old chateau on the out-
skirts of Sarajevo. There was no gymnasium and no Phys Ed
program. I think all the school had was a ping-pong table."

"There were two tables."

"There's something! Suzanne was very good at ping-
pong."

"Mom!"

"Last spring she won a championship."

"Good for you," Mr. Mulroney forced what was supposed
to be an encouraging smile. He was trying to be nice. I
knew that, but on some visceral level, I didn't like his smile
as I didn't like him. I knew I was safe, but I couldn't help
feeling that I was facing something evil.

"I don't want people to know," I said. I was pouting,
behaving childishly.

"So you've never played volleyball or done any track and
field? I think they're still doing volleyball now and they
finish the year with track."

"No," I said. "I've never done track and field."

"Well, you'll get a chance to try it here. I'll speak to a
couple of the teachers and we'll have a schedule for you on
Monday. Perhaps you could come in as well," he said, turning to my mom. "There will be a few papers to fill out and
sign."

"Thank you. What time would you like us here?"

"How about 8:30? Did you say Sarajevo? Where the fight-
ing broke out?"

"Yes," said my mother. "Good-bye for now." She wasn't
going to elaborate. She acted as if the last week had never
happened to us.

That's what I remember of my first meeting with Joseph
Mulroney. I didn't really meet him again until after my final
exam, so that he was the first person I saw in that school,

and the last. In between, I hardly saw him at all. Once or twice I caught a glimpse of him at the end of a hallway, or crossing the lobby, but he didn't seem to be around the school very much, which was fine with me. He had been perfectly nice with us. It had not been an interrogation at the hands of the Serbs. We hadn't been beaten or threatened with rape and disfigurement. I told myself that first impressions can be misleading, but I never quite erased that first image I had of him, as a stern, grey-clad Serbian officer.

On Monday, when we went to the school, my mom and I were met by Mme Ducharme, who was the vice principal, and who turned out to be very nice. The first couple of days, I saw her several times in the hallways and she always smiled and stopped to ask how I was doing: was I finding my way around? Was the Math similar to what I was used to? Had I met one student or another? It was Mme Ducharme who arranged things to allow me to write all my O-Levels at the school, instead of going to Montreal, where I had to go to do my Art exam.

My mom stayed with the secretary to fill out some papers while Mme Ducharme walked me around part of the school and introduced me to a couple of teachers we met in the hallways: to Mr. Nichols, who taught Math, and whom I really came to like in the short time I had him, and also to Miss Normandin, who was the first and only gym teacher I had in my entire high school career. Then the school started filling up with kids and she brought me to my homeroom where I met Mrs. Mulroney.

I had no particular feelings about Mrs. Mulroney when I first met her. I certainly had no visceral reaction to her. Of course, after I'd been in her class a while, that changed. Looking back, I see her as a reincarnation of Lady Macbeth, a twisted soul driven by the desire to see her daughter crowned.

It was Manon who told me that Magdalene was the Mulroneys' daughter.

"Didn't you know?" she asked me, coming out of English class one day. Her tone of voice, the look she gave me, the shrug of her shoulders, all made me feel naïve. But it wasn't me she was mad at. This was not very long after I arrived. Much as my first day of high school in Canada made me feel like the foreigner I was, it didn't take long for me to feel as if I'd been there almost forever. Although there were still surprises, and finding out who was related to whom was certainly one of them.

At Miss Wallace's, the entire school body had probably been only marginally greater than the number of kids in one of my classes here. But at Miss Wallace's, we were from all over the place—I was the only Canadian but there were three Americans, several Brits, and kids from half a dozen countries in Europe and the Middle East. Here, it seemed that every other kid turned out to be someone's second cousin. There weren't any family resemblances that I could notice, but it figured that Magdalene (who was called Maggie by everyone except her mother) would turn out to be Mrs. Mulroney's daughter.

Mrs. Mulroney wasn't just my home room teacher. Except for Math and French—and Phys Ed—she taught all the other Grade 11 courses, so I saw a lot of her, and her daughter.

I don't think it's necessarily easy for a teacher to be fair, to be equitable. In fact it's not easy for anybody to be fair. We all seem to be born with a bias or prejudice of some sort, even for seemingly inconsequential things. I've read that red and yellow cars are more likely to be stopped for speeding than cars of any other colour; that sports teams with black uniforms draw more penalties; that tall men rise up the corporate ladder more easily and quickly than their shorter colleagues. Yet, there are certain professions of which we expect fairness. For example, we expect judges to be fair and we expect teachers to be fair.

So far, thank goodness, I have had no experience with judges, so I can't say from personal experience; although my optimism on that question is guarded. I have been told by a few people that it's a wise thing, regardless of the dispute, to settle it without going to court. And of course, there's that charming English expression: The Law is an Ass.

As for teachers, well, they're human. I speak with firsthand knowledge. I did a fifth year at the Nova Scotia College of Art and Design because I thought it wise to have a profession to fall back on. I never became an Art teacher, but I do have some classroom experience. I did some supply work a decade ago and more recently I've been going into classrooms as an invited (and paid) guest to do workshops and talk about my day job, which is illustrating children's books. I've met a lot of teachers, and many of them I see as admirable people. I've no doubt that most of them strive to be fair. But there are exceptions.

Mary Mulroney was an exception. She was such an exception that, in retrospect, I think if I'd known the situation I might have opted to sit with the Grade 10 classes, or perhaps even chosen to go to the French school ten kilometres away.

When I was quite young, I was surprised when one of my brothers told me one day, "Dad will never operate on you. He'll never operate on any of us. If we ever need an operation, we'll go to another surgeon, not Dad." This bit of information made me cry. I took it to mean that my father didn't care about us.

The truth was just the opposite. "It's because I love you that I would never operate on you," my father explained.

"Doctors never treat members of their own family, let alone operate on them. When you love someone, when you're emotionally attached to someone, you lose your objectivity; your judgment can become clouded. You can make mistakes, serious mistakes."

"Imagine what could happen if I were operating on your heart. I could start thinking that this was *your* heart. Not any heart, but *your* heart. I might get tears in my eyes. My vision would be blurred. I wouldn't see what I was doing. I could make a mistake. Instead of saving your life, I could end up taking your life. Your heart is very special to me, so special that I wouldn't be able to see just your heart. I'd be seeing all of you and thinking of you. I wouldn't be focussed on the operation. I could make a mistake. Do you understand what I'm saying?"

Mrs. Mulroney had the blurred vision my father had spoken of, and it wasn't at all corrected by her stylish glasses. The only kid in the classroom she ever saw was Magdalene. Or maybe that's not quite right. The only person in the classroom that she cared about was Magdalene. The rest of us she saw as either beneficial or harmful to her daughter. In all of Mrs. Mulroney's classes, we sat in groups of four or five. Maggie's group was always at the front of the class, to the right of her mother's desk. You could tell how you stood with Mrs. Mulroney by where she assigned you to sit. If you were one of the three or four kids at Maggie's table, it was because you were seen as potentially helpful to Maggie, although you probably had more friends if you sat anywhere else in the class.

Where I noticed it most, and noticed it first, was in English, which here they called Language Arts—a term I still find pretentious. As far as I could tell, it paid little attention to language and none to art. At least, that was the way Mrs. Mulroney taught it.

Just as colour on a canvass can be made darker by placing a lighter tone beside it, I think I saw Mrs. Mulroney as an absolute horror because at Miss Wallace's, for the last two years, I had had Mr. Nado for English. We called him Mr. Nado but his name really was Peter Nadofanskovich, and despite the Russian name, he was from York, in the north of England. He was married to a very beautiful woman who was working in Sarajevo as a translator. He was trying to write poetry and was teaching half days at Miss Wallace's to "pay for the candles" as he put it. He was relatively young. Sometimes, we thought he was a little strange, but he was without a doubt a phenomenal teacher.

He was very meticulous about vocabulary, about the nuances between words. For example, he'd challenge us to define the difference between synonyms, like joy and happiness. Sometimes, he'd write a word on the board and talk about it for half an hour, not just about what it meant, but the origins of the word and how its meaning had evolved— like the word awful which originally meant wondrous or inspiring and then came to mean horrible but, now changed to awesome, it again has a positive connotation. When we got back our written assignments, there would often be pointed questions in the margin, "Is this really the word you want?"

He gave life to ideas. Like most kids, I had no particular interest in parsing sentences, but with him, learning English was genuinely interesting. He made it into a game of sorts, a puzzle to sort out and put together. He often talked about the solidly constructed sentence, and the phrase still brings to mind the cross-braced two-by-fours of a house under construction, which he once drew on the blackboard.

What I'm most grateful for is that he taught me to write. Looking back with adult eyes that have seen a few classrooms, I realize that Mr. Nado had an immeasurable advantage compared to almost all teachers in Canada. He had only five of us doing O-Level Composition at Miss Wallace's and only four doing Literature. Still, he gave us interesting things to write about, and we wrote a lot. Sometimes, he'd start class by pulling something out of his pocket, or out of his briefcase; we'd look at it and then write about the strange stone or odd pencil sharpener or whatever it was that he'd brought in. He'd give us unusual writing assignments. For example, he'd write some words on the blackboard and we'd have to incorporate all the words in a short paragraph on some odd topic or theme. Or he'd have us imagine ourselves to be an inanimate object, or an animal, or a character in a book and write as that thing or person.

What really came home to me, when I was in Mrs. Mulroney's Language Arts class, was the way that Mr. Nado corrected our work. Any time you got your paper back, there were always tons of comments in fine black ink in Mr. Nado's small, neat script. It was as if he was beside you and reading your paper with you. There would be questions in the margins or remarks on one thing or another. Sometimes, he'd end up writing almost as much as you'd written. But one thing he didn't do, or at least, he didn't often do, is grade the work. Sometimes he might say, "That could get you a 1," or "Make errors like that and you'll be lucky to get a 6." What he would do, really, was tell you what you'd done well and then tell you where your work might improve, and how to start to improve it.

Unlike Mr. Nado, Mrs. Mulroney was stingy with her comments. She might write "Good!" at the end of your paper, or "Watch your handwriting" or "Check your spelling," but you always got the feeling that, at best, she'd skimmed over your work without really reading any of it. Yet everything was graded—your percentage boldly circled in red ink.

We didn't do that much for her, at least not compared to what I was used to doing, and as I said, I can understand that. I've seen oversized classes and I can understand how a teacher, especially an English teacher, would be inclined not to give many assignments. Correcting a paper can be a lot of work and Mrs. Mulroney was certainly not the only teacher in the country to skim through student assignments superficially and cavalierly.

Being with Mrs. Mulroney was like suddenly finding myself plodding along on a narrow, dusty track on an aged donkey after having pranced through open fields on a thoroughbred. I remember Mrs. Mulroney as someone who talked a lot but said little. Mostly, she talked about herself. In her stories, others were always asking her advice, or perhaps ignoring her advice, but inevitably, her advice was golden. The individual who approached her was either munificently rewarded for heeding her words or fell into ruin for failing to do so.

In class, she was a teacher who had what those in the profession call "good discipline." She did not smile easily, and when she did it was an artificial smile. Her facial muscles rarely went beyond the range of stern to serious. She had a strong voice which vibrated with the tone of unquestionable authority. It was also an unpleasant voice, like an especially raucous crow. She wielded great power in her classroom and you could tell that she enjoyed flexing her metaphoric muscle. Born in Bela Palanca or Cuprija, she would have been equally intimidating as a Serbian prison guard.

Magdalene wasn't one of the first kids I noticed in class. She was sufficiently nondescript that, in a sea of new faces and personalities, hers hadn't stood out. I think the first thing I noticed about her was her favoured status. She'd been called on to respond to some silly question and was given an inordinate amount of praise for spouting out what sounded like a banal answer. My first impression of her was that she was a well-dressed, middle-class girl of my age who—when I learned who they were—bore little resemblance to either of her parents.

Her favoured status, or the degree to which she was favoured, was made clear to me towards the end of year. When I arrived, I'd been placed at one table and then a couple of weeks later, I'd been moved to Maggie's table, to start what Mrs. Mulroney announced as the last and most important assignment of the year. Mrs. Mulroney's assignments were always collaborative efforts. Each table was a team and the team worked on the assignment together. In this case, we had to prepare a "response" to a book the class had been reading for the last two months. (I don't remember the title, but it was a pulp novel, one of those "best sellers" that's predictable to read and easy to forget.) We had to document our exploration of the book, which meant we had to take notes and prepare short drafts that we'd pass around and peer edit and so accumulate what was called a portfolio. The idea was to hand in a manila folder filled with a paper trail that led from initial discussions to a formal response, which was nothing more than a short essay.

All this took the better part of two weeks. When we got our papers back, all of us at our table had marks in the mid-seventies—except for Maggie. She got back a paper with ninety-six percent circled in red. I was startled because, during all the time we'd spent on the assignment, she hadn't really done much of anything. She hadn't said anything insightful and the drafts she wrote were as dull as anybody else's.

I found it a bizarre exercise. With Mr. Nado, writing had been about personal engagement. It was about articulating a thought. In Mrs. Mulroney's class, writing was a team activity. It was composition by committee; but the compensation was by consanguinity. The grading was blatantly biased.

I was an outsider. It didn't concern me. It was the end of the school year. And if I had noticed this, so too must have many others. My grandmother listed all the reasons that it was best to quietly accept my situation. "It's too bad," she said. "It's very sad to see nepotism. But the best thing you can do is to focus on your own work. You're lucky because this doesn't really affect you. This woman won't be grading any of your exams."

As it turned out, thanks to Mme Ducharme, I was able to write almost all my exams at my new school. "Your A-Level Art you'll have to do at Marianopolis in Montreal," she explained. "But we can administer all the O-Level exams right here. While your classmates are writing their exams, you'll be in the same place but writing exams of your own."

What I remember about the last few weeks of school was that almost everybody was all worked up by the thought of the graduation prom. If the high school leaving exams were a concern, it was only to the teachers. As for the kids, the exams were no big deal. Almost everybody seemed to take it for granted that he or she would be in *Cégep* in the fall or at work on a farm or in a factory.

What everybody was going on about was the prom. At a certain point, Manon approached me and asked me if I was interested in going.

"I know you just got here," she said, "but if you're shy about going because you don't have a date, I know a boy who'd be happy to ask you."

"I don't know," I said. "I may not be here at the end of June." The youngest of my three big brothers, Charlie, was graduating from Oxford at the end of June. I knew that mom and I would be going to the ceremony for sure. Besides, our lives were still speckled with lots of uncertainties. My dad had come to Canada for a week and then flown back to England, even though, the way my parents had talked, it seemed that we might be staying here in Canada. So I was being truthful when I said I really wasn't sure if I would be around for the prom.

But Manon was partly right. I wasn't at all sure that I'd feel comfortable going to a prom. As Manon had said, I'd just arrived. I was still a stranger. These kids, if they weren't related, had been together in the same class, some of them, since they'd started kindergarten. More than that, for almost everybody, it was an event for couples, and I wasn't sure that I wanted to go on a first date, almost a blind date, wearing heels and a strapless gown.

In the end, I had a couple of reasons not to go. The Friday of the prom, the second last Friday of the month, was also the day I had to be in Montreal to do my A-Level Art exam. Then, a day later, my mom and I would be flying to London for Charlie's graduation, among other things.

The incident that brought me back into Joseph Mulroney's office happened on Thursday, the day before the prom. It was a very hot afternoon and I was writing my very last O-Level exam which was French. I had made the mistake of declining my grandmother's offer of a ride to school. Normally, the walk—less than twenty minutes—was invigorating. I was wearing sandals and a simple, light summer dress, but the sun was much hotter than I'd thought. I was annoyed because I'd worked up a sweat. Then, as I was approaching the front doors of the school, going up the steps that lead to them, I somehow stumbled and, even though I didn't know it then, I broke the baby toe of my left foot. (Several hours later, a doctor confirmed it was broken and told me that it would have to heal itself.)

My exam was to start at 12:30 and end, at the latest, at 3:30. The others were writing math, from 1:15 to 3:15. I hobbled into the small gym which was filled with rows of desks and chairs. Mr. Nichols was supervising because he was the Grade 11 math teacher. He noticed I was limping.

"I hope you'll be ok," he said, and because he was trying to make me feel better, he joked, "At least it's not your right hand."

He asked me if I minded going to the very back. "This way the others won't disturb you as much when they come in or when they leave. And nobody will accidentally bump your foot."

He handed me the examination papers, made sure I had two pens, and left me to start my exam. He returned a few minutes later with a bag of ice wrapped in a white hand towel which he handed to me silently, pointing to my throbbing baby toe. I spent the exam trying to do some French between waves of pain. I would use my right foot to very gingerly push the cold towel against my aching toe and then, a few minutes later, slide my freezing foot away. At one point Mr. Nichols brought me a second towel-wrapped ice pack and took the first one—now melted—away.

At some point, and it must have been after Mr. Nichols brought me the second towel, it happened. I had just raised my head to stretch my neck and shoulders and my eye caught a flutter of movement. Just ahead of me, in the middle of the aisle, I saw a paper float to the floor.

I was sitting in the very last seat closest to the wall. Two desks in front of me sat Tamara Lockwell and beside her, in the second row from the wall, sat Maggie. Three seats in front of Maggie sat Manon. The four of us were the only ones in that corner of the gym which was four-fifths empty because, except for my French, Math was the only exam being written that afternoon.

I saw the paper float downwards, swaying like a jerky pendulum, and settle on the hardwood floor half way between Maggie and her best friend, Tamara. I had not seen where it came from; but I did see, half a moment later, Maggie's right leg reach out and try to touch the paper. It was an awkward motion and her leg wasn't quite long enough. She started to make a second attempt to reach the paper with her foot when I saw Tamara's head and shoulders make a short quarter turn to look behind. For one of those moments which feels long but is probably very short, her eye caught mine. Tamara quickly swung back but she took the briefest fraction of a second to wag her head as if to say no to the girl beside her. Maggie's leg retreated casually back under its desk, as if perhaps it had been innocently stretching.

The paper lay inert on the gym floor for no more than two or three minutes. Mr. Nichols was invigilating the exams with a second teacher whom I didn't know although I had seen her around. It was she who, perhaps because her invisible antennae had picked up some unusual vibration, strolled down our aisle a few minutes later. She picked up the paper as if it were a basketball or volleyball which had innocently rolled out of the storage cupboard. She didn't look at anyone and glanced at the scrap in her hand as if it were of no more interest than a week-old advertising flyer.

A few minutes later, a grim Mr. Nichols, holding the same scrap of paper, marched down the aisle and stopped pretty much where it had landed. He stared at the bent heads below him for a long couple of minutes before spinning on his heels and marching back up the aisle.

Despite the few minutes I'd lost watching this scene unfold, and despite the recurring waves of throbbing pain from my baby toe, I finished my exam not too long after the last of the math kids left the gym.

As I gave my papers to Mr. Nichols he asked, "Were you able to write your exam just the same?"

"I think so."

"Good. Do I have all your papers? These will be mailed this afternoon. I'm sorry to ask you because I'm sure you want to get home and have your foot looked at, but would you come to Mr. Mulroney's office? Something happened. I know it doesn't involve you in any way but he wants to speak with you as well."

Limping gamely, I followed Mr. Nichols out of the gym, across the lobby and down the hall to the principal's office.

"Is there someone you can call to come get you?" he asked as we crossed the lobby.

"Yes, I'd like to call my grandmother."

"I'll have the secretary call her for you."

He knocked perfunctorily on the closed office door and I followed him in. Mr. Mulroney was seated behind his desk. Maggie and Tamara were seated in the two plush chairs in which my mother and I had sat a few months before, while Manon stood near them. The girls, thin-lipped and tense, turned towards us as we came in. Mr. Nichols closed the door behind us.

"Something very serious seems to have happened," Mr. Mulroney began. "Someone, it seems, brought a crib sheet into the math exam. These three girls, Mr. Nichols has told me, were all near the spot where this crib sheet was found. I've seen these three girls together and I've heard

what they had to say. In a few minutes, I'm going to speak
to each of them again, individually this time, and ask them
a few more questions. You were also near the spot where the
paper was found. I know you had nothing to do with this
but it's still important that I question you. Mr. Nichols told
me you hurt your foot this afternoon? I'll start with you so
you can get home and get it looked at."

Mr. Nichols and the three girls left the office.

"You can sit," he said to me.

He said it nicely but I was suddenly tense and stiff, hardly
able to move. I limped two steps to the nearest chair and
sat uncomfortably.

"How are your exams going? You're writing exams that
come all the way from England, I think?"

"Yes, my O-Levels."

"Do you have many more to write?"

"No. This was my last one."

"And what exam were you writing?"

"French."

"Did it go well?"

"I hope so."

"You say this was your last exam?"

"My last O-Level. I have to do my Art exam tomorrow,
but it's in Montreal."

"So, we won't see you here anymore? Where did your
mother say you were going to school next year?"

"Edinburgh, but it's not certain yet."

"In Scotland?"

"Yes, in Scotland. But it's not certain yet."

"Are you spending the summer here?"

"No, or rather, I don't know. We're flying to England on
Monday..."

"This Monday?"

"This Monday, yes. We're going to be there for a couple of weeks and after that I don't know."

"Well, I hope you have a good trip. Now, about this afternoon. Have you said anything to Mr. Nichols?"

"No."

"Nothing at all? Did Mr. Nichols ask you anything?"

"No. He just asked me to follow him to the office."

"So, you didn't speak to him about anything at all?"

"No, just to call my grandmother to come and get me."

He seemed momentarily at a loss for words, as if he had to think what to do next.

"I have to ask you this," he said, "just as a formality. Did you bring this paper into the gym this afternoon?"

The question startled me so much I almost laughed. A sound came out of me and I tried to cover it as a cough. "No, of course not," I said.

With a very straight face, as if he had asked a serious question, he said, "No, I didn't think so. I'll let you go now to get that foot looked at."

I was startled and it may have taken me a moment to move but, as I rose to go, he really surprised me.

"It was nice to have you in our school," he said, rising and coming around his desk towards me. "I hope you learned a lot."

Then he reached forward and I realized he wanted to shake my hand.

I had barely stepped out of his office when I spotted my grandmother at the far end of the hallway. I passed by the others who were standing along the wall near the door. I nodded goodbye to Manon who looked back at me with strangely frightened eyes and said thank you to Mr. Nichols in little more than a whisper. The other two girls, Maggie and Tamara, were looking away as I went by them.

And that was it.

I disappeared as suddenly as I had arrived and, for more than a decade, the story remained unfinished.

Not that I didn't think about it. In my mind, I would go back and replay my last meeting with Joseph Mulroney over and over again. What at first made no sense at all, eventually made me feel duped, and taken advantage of, and especially it made me feel worried and apprehensive for Manon. I knew that whatever else Joseph Mulroney's inquiry might find, I was absolutely certain that it would find his own daughter perfectly innocent of any involvement whatsoever with the crib sheet. Several times, over the years, I found myself back at my grandmother's—and then my parents'— place for a few days at a time. Once or twice I thought of calling Manon and then it seemed that so much time had passed that it didn't really matter any more. In the scale of things, Joseph Mulroney's transgression, however much it bothered me, was laughably trivial. Still, it stayed with me even as life went on.

Despite my broken baby toe (which swelled to remarkable proportions and displayed an impressive palette of colours) I sat my Art exam the next day in Montreal and did quite well. Wearing an oversized and unmatched shoe, I went to Charlie's graduation and visited Edinburgh, but that fall I enrolled at the Nova Scotia College of Art and Design. This permitted me to live at home for two more years; my parents, after more than a decade of wanderlust had opted to return to Canada and had landed in Dartmouth. Much as they liked Nova Scotia, they moved two years later so my mother could go from babying a daughter to nursing a mother. After my grandmother passed away, my parents stayed here because the house was comfortable, and convenient for my father, who had only a short half-hour commute to his hospital across the river in Ottawa. Then, when my father suffered his first stroke, I came here with the intention of helping out my mom for a few weeks. To my surprise, I never left.

It was at the hospital that I bumped into Manon, a day or two after my father had his stroke. I had just arrived from Vancouver and driven a rental car directly from the Ottawa airport to the hospital. I was walking down a corridor when I saw a face coming towards me that I couldn't quite identify although it looked familiar.

"Suzanne from Sarajevo?" she said.

"Manon?"

She was now a doctor at the same hospital where my father had suddenly gone from being a dispenser of medical services to a consumer of them. An hour later, we sat over two cups of bad coffee and stale muffins.

"That's your dad? I'm so sorry. Everyone is," she said when I explained why I was there. We exchanged our stories: she was happily married to a stay-at-home architect who was raising their two children. She had gone into medicine and become an anaesthesiologist. She had frequently worked with my father. Inevitably, we talked about our final exam.

"I can't believe it!" she said after listening to me. "I always thought I owed my life to you. I called your grandmother's place several times. I wanted to thank you because I was sure that you had saved my skin.

"I was really scared that afternoon. I finished my exam and, as I was handing it in, Mr. Nichols asked me to follow him to the office. I couldn't understand why I was wanted at the office, but the moment I walked in and saw Maggie and Tamara sitting in front of Mulroney, I knew that I was in big trouble. And I was scared. I'd never liked Mulroney, either of the Mulroneys. I had never had anything to do with him, but I thought she was a witch. But right then, when I walked into that office, I was physically frightened, and when he asked Mr. Nichols to go and get you I was desperately searching my mind for clues as to what this could all be about. And the moment Mr. Nichols closed the door behind him, I realized that, whatever was going on, the only person who might possibly have protected me had just left.

"He looked at me for several seconds, staring at me so that I felt there was something wrong with me and I couldn't look back at him. 'Something was found in the examination room,' he finally said. 'Close to where you were sitting. Would you take a look at it?' He handed me a piece of paper—half a sheet of lined paper torn out of a binder. It was creased and a little crumpled. It was full of math. And then he started questioning me. He kept his voice soft, but his questions came one after the other and with each one I felt more and more as if I had something to hide. 'Have you seen this paper before? Can you explain how it came to be near your desk? Could you tell me what some of the writing is? Are you sure you haven't seen this paper before?' Finally I put the paper back on his desk and I told him it wasn't mine and I didn't know anything about it. I don't know how I did it, but I said it to his face, staring right at him. And I was the only one he spoke to, as if Maggie and Tamara weren't even there.

"I don't know what would have happened next if you hadn't arrived. I knew I was in big trouble even though I was innocent. I was just praying that you might be able to say something because if you didn't, I knew that I was the one who would be blamed.

"Maggie's parents wanted one thing for their daughter, that she graduate at the top of her class. She couldn't be caught cheating on a final exam, which might even mean losing her year. And her father wouldn't be likely to let anything happen to Tamara either, because for the last five years Tamara had been Maggie's bodyguard. This left me as the guilty party.

"I could see all that as clearly as if it had been written on the wall. But I grew less scared when I was waiting out in the hall," she continued. "For one thing Mr. Nichols was there and somehow I felt good about that. As I stood there, I grew more and more determined that I was going to fight. I was ready to demand that they bring in a handwriting expert or demand a lie detector test. Don't laugh. I remember those ideas going through my head. Math was my best subject, always had been. You know how Maggie always got the highest marks in Language Arts class? Well, that never happened in Math. She was scraping by. Whereas, if I wasn't at the top of the class, I was always near the top. I was the last person in that room who needed a crib sheet of any kind, and I knew Mr. Nichols would back me up on that. Still, I was afraid when I walked back into his office. As you can probably guess, I was the one who went in last. After you came out of the office, Mulroney called his daughter in. After maybe five minutes he called Tamara in even though Maggie hadn't come out. He was a little longer with Tamara, or maybe it just felt longer. Then he called me in.

"I remember being startled that neither Maggie nor Tamara were there. It took me a minute to realize that they would have left by the door that led to his secretary's office. They would have gone out through the main office and into the lobby and out the front door without seeing or being seen by anyone.

"He told me to sit and I felt stiff and uncomfortable. He took a long time to start talking. He leaned forward with his elbows on the desk and his hands together as if he were praying. Anyway, for a moment, because he hadn't said a word, I thought he was going to close his eyes and pray.

"He didn't pray, and he didn't bombard me with more accusatory questions, which is what I was expecting. What he did was lecture me. He talked, in a serious, fatherly voice, about the gravity of cheating and the importance of hard work and effort. It was all platitudes and I couldn't understand where he was going. I kept wondering when he was going to say, 'You did it!' but he didn't. He talked about reasonable doubt, and how he would not want an innocent person to be punished. He said that, despite what one of the other girls had said, he could not be sure beyond reasonable doubt who had brought the crib sheet into the exam. And at that point, in my head, I wanted to give you such a hug to thank you. I was sure that you must have seen something and told him. I don't know if any of this showed on my face. It must have.

"All of a sudden, out of the blue, he asked me if I had cheated on the exam and would I be willing to swear on a Bible that I hadn't? I said yes, I would swear on a Bible that I hadn't cheated and that was it, he dismissed me, and sent me out through Wendy's office.

"He was a smart man. He implied I was the guilty party without ever actually saying it, and then let me know that I should be grateful that he was lenient and forgiving. The truth is, all I felt was relief. At that point, all I cared was that I wasn't being blamed.

"And all this time, in my heart, I've been saying thank you to you," she said. Then her pager must have gone off because she reached into her pocket and said, "I have to go. We're all thinking of your dad. He's getting the very best care. It's remarkable, sometimes, the extent to which people can recover from a stroke."

My dad, who had been so remarkable all his life wasn't so this time. His recovery was slow and limited. He suffered a second and then a third stroke before dying unexpectedly and quietly in his sleep a week after his seventieth birthday.

Manon, who had been my father's colleague, became again, and remains, a close friend. Her story answered my questions while raising others. At graduation, both Tamara and Maggie collected their diplomas. Maggie, as expected, took the top academic prize. According to Manon, there were a lot of kids, and a lot of adults as well, who didn't applaud. Mr. Nichols did not return to the school the following September. It seems he's now teaching at a private school somewhere near Toronto. Both Manon and I are curious to hear his story, and we occasionally promise ourselves that we will look him up one of these days although neither of us has yet done so.

I COULD TELL THAT LARA WAS GLAD TO BE HOME, and so was I. We had walked much further than we normally do. From Craig's field, we followed our path through scrub brush to the Cemetery Road, but instead of taking our usual downhill stroll, I surprised Lara by turning up the hill. As we reached the crest of Cemetery Road, the sun evaporated the remaining mist. In no more than a few minutes, the sky became almost blindingly blue. The air would no doubt grow heavier through the afternoon, but at that moment it felt crisp and we could see into the folds of the Gatineau hills. We walked the last half hour of our five-mile jaunt under an increasingly hot sun.

இ

I fill Lara's water bowl and pour a tall glass for myself. I drink half the glass at once, refill it and bring it with me to the studio. I reflect on how fortunate I am. My job (or my profession—where is Mr. Nado when I need him?) is to render with pencils, or ink or paints, the images that a writer has previously created with words. I encounter any number of difficulties and problems in my line of work, but most are of a technical nature and can be overcome or corrected or solved by careful application of my art. The tasks presented to me are ultimately straightforward, as are the people I work with: authors, editors, publishers, printers. I have met no Mulroneys in the course of my work.

I'm starting a new set of drawings this morning and, as with any project, I begin by tidying up my work space. I am not messy by nature but the by-product of every project is a certain quantity of clutter. I turn on the radio and eventually I hear again the news item that set me off earlier in the morning. The second time round Mulroney's words illicit nothing more than a snort from me. I attack the clutter with renewed energy and quite suddenly, my workspace is, if not clean to my mother's standards, at least amply cleared for my next project.

For a moment, I wonder what moves such men—well educated and blessed with intelligence—to become tawdry cheats?

Perhaps I shouldn't ask, for I have work to do.

I pick up a pencil and the new manuscript. The text is a piece that I've looked at once already, briefly, a few weeks ago, when it came in the mail. Then I was comfortably settled in my reading nook. Not so now. I perch myself at my drafting table and, pencil in hand, I start to read *Muffet's Adventure*.

The Sleigh

Malachy woke up to the smell of wood smoke from the kitchen. His first thought was one of surprise, surprise that no one had come to wake him up and rouse him out of bed. It was still dark and he had no way of knowing how late, or how early, it might be. The bed, which he shared with his cousin, Joe, was no longer warm for Joe had already risen to start the day. Malachy stretched out his legs and his toes touched the bricks at the foot of the bed. As he expected, they were cool, almost cold to the touch. Cold and rough, the edges almost sharp enough to slice his foot. To think that at night the same bricks, even wrapped in flannel cloth, were so hot that his toes couldn't touch them for more than a few seconds.

He wondered why no one had roused him and he lay still for several minutes, listening to the sounds from downstairs. It was hard to understand, because it seemed as if it was only his aunt in the kitchen. There were no voices, only the occasional sound of her footsteps or of the firebox creaking open and the dull thud of a block of wood thrown on the fire.

The bed got no warmer and here and there he could feel sharp splinters of straw poking through the threadbare burlap and his flannel nightdress. He pushed off the heavy blankets and rolled himself out of bed. The floorboards were cold on his feet. He dressed quickly and, still barefoot, climbed down the ladder into the relative warmth of the kitchen, the large, main room of the small house.

"Good morning, Aunt," he said.

His Aunt Rachel had her back to him and she did not turn to look at him.

"'Bout time you were up," she said. "It's almost light out. I need water. Better fill up both pails."

Malachy went to the stove and from the cord strung above it took down a pair of heavy wool socks. The warmth near the stove was like a call to linger. The stove had clearly been lit for some time for the rough wool was not just dry but warm—almost hot—to the touch. With his still-cold fingers he squeezed the material as if to take as much heat from it as he could. He tried to stretch out all his movements, removing the socks slowly and one at a time from the cord on which they hung.

He glanced at his aunt before taking a chance and moving a chair a little closer to the stove. He sat on it and waited a long minute before pulling on one sock and then the other. Then he sat still a moment longer, aware that his failure to move quickly might earn him the sharp edge of his aunt's tongue. He noticed that the kettle on the stove was releasing its first preliminary wisps of vapour and that the short-handled wooden spoon was protruding at a slant from the porridge pot. He wondered if the porridge hadn't already been made, and if there'd be any for him. He looked at the kettle again and it came to him that it had already been emptied once this morning. There were dirty dishes on the sideboard near the basin as if Joe and Uncle Sean had already eaten. Again, he silently questioned where his cousin and uncle might be.

Malachy stood and on warm-soled feet made his way towards the door. He could tell from the frost on the windows that it was another cold day. As he tied the laces of his worn boots, one of them snapped. He knew better than to say anything to his aunt. As quickly as he could, he reworked the broken lace, struggling to pass it through the eyelets. In the end, he was able to tie on his boot with the two shortened laces so that only four of the eyelets remained empty, and the boot, already a few sizes too big, did not fall off his foot. He wrapped his scarf around his neck and then slipped on the worn jacket that had been given him as a winter coat. He pulled his woollen toque down over his ears and reached for his mitts. Of all his winter apparel, it was his mitts he treasured the most. They were almost new and, even though they were a few sizes too big for his small hands, they were wonderful mitts: heavy, dark leather lined on the inside with warm felt. They were gone. In fact, there were no mitts at all on the small shelf reserved for mitts and scarves and hats, not even the old green ones that were full of holes.

"Haven't gone yet?" his aunt yelled. "You should have been back by now. Didn't I tell ya to go get me two buckets of water, ya lazy good-for-nothing!"

She took two steps towards him but Malachy knew—he didn't know how, but he knew—that she wasn't going to cuff him. Still, he made himself smaller and avoided looking directly at her. She stopped, still a few paces from the door, and scowled at him for a moment.

"If yer not back with them two buckets in five minutes time there's no breakfast for ya! Is that clear?"

Malachy meekly nodded. He knew, at that moment, that there was no porridge left for him. It would take him almost five minutes just to walk to the spring. He picked up one of the wooden pails with his left hand, lifted the door latch with his right and pushed open the door. Less quickly than he normally would, he took the second pail with his right hand and stepped out of the door and into the cold. Sometimes he closed the door by nudging it with his elbow, or even by leaning into it with his shoulder. This morning, he let it swing half open for an extra few seconds and then kicked it closed with his left boot, the one with the lace still intact.

The cold air closed his nostrils and burned his throat. He put both pails down and pulled his arms up in the sleeves of his coat as far as he could so there would be a bit of sleeve between the skin of his fingers and the rope handles of the pails.

He stepped off the porch and, before he had taken three steps, he understood what had happened. The sleigh was gone, its tell-tale traces in the dust of snow leading away from the house and turning right onto the Waterloo Road. Malachy stopped dead in his tracks and bent over as if he'd been kicked in the stomach. He could feel tears welling up in his eyes. He felt a pain he could neither describe nor bear, and if he had, at that moment, been given the option of death, he would instantly have taken it.

When he finally straightened his back and started shuffling towards the spring, he moved as if walking in his sleep, hardly conscious of his actions. In his mind, the same phrase repeated itself over and over and over: they went without me.

It was only on the way back from the spring, his fingertips frozen, his arms sore, his left pant leg stiff with ice from water which had splashed over the bucket's rim, that the simple phrase expanded. And when it did, it was like the expansion of gases in the firing chamber of a rifle. It was an explosion. It was a short lifetime of pain and hurt and anger and injustice that filled his mind with sound and smoke and fury. The death of his mother and then the disappearance of his father; the sudden separation from his sisters and brother; his Aunt Rachel and Uncle Sean who never missed an opportunity to let him know what a burden he was. And today, a Saturday he had been looking forward to for months, a Saturday he had been promised, a Saturday on which he would again see, even if only for a brief few minutes, his sister Colleen and maybe Siobhan as well, a Saturday...

Then he was home. Not his home, but what he was forced to call home. He almost walked past the house, his mind was so full of confusion. He stopped a moment and put the pails down. He had no idea how long ago his aunt had told him five minutes or no breakfast, but it suddenly seemed a long time. The sky was growing light and there was already a bit of traffic on the road. He hadn't been alone at the spring fetching water.

Still on the road, where the drive entered towards the house, he put the pails down and flexed his fingers to bring back some blood. He clasped his hands together to try to give them some warmth. He stood for a moment staring at the house as if he had never seen it before. Then he saw his aunt at the window, pulling the white transparent curtain to one side to look out. To look for him. And then his eyes met hers and he saw her scowl with anger and impatience and a moment later she was at the door, yelling at him.

He bent his knees and reached down with his cold hands to pick up his load and at the same moment heard the yelling stop and the door bang closed. He straightened again, but without the pails. Then, his body acting entirely of its own accord, as if it belonged to someone else, he tipped one pail, and then the other, and with only half a load, walked the last dozen paces to the house.

His aunt was nowhere near the door when he came in and put down the two, half-full pails. She was at the stove, throwing in another block of wood. She banged the firebox closed and turned on him, her eyes as red as flames.

"Where have ya bin, ya ragamuffin? All this time I bin waiting for ya. Git those pails over here. But git yer boots off first."

Malachy, and again it felt as if his body belonged to someone else, stood stock still and stared at her as if she were a total stranger he'd never before seen.

"Well, hurry up!" she screamed. "I ain't got all day. What's wrong with ya?"

Malachy heard himself speak and his words surprised him as much as they did his Aunt Rachel.

"Here's your water," he said and then kicked one and then the second pail over, spilling the precious water over the kitchen floor.

He didn't hear her words and he was strangely unmoved by her rage. Even when she started to move towards him with her hand upraised, he didn't cringe or flinch. He was surprised to find a broom in his hands and to see her stop with a look of incomprehension on her face.

For a moment, the two stood apart in silence, separated by the thin film of water that was spreading slowly across the floor.

And then she spoke. "When your uncle gets home…"

Malachy threw the broom at her, spun on his heels and went out the door.

It took him several minutes to realize what had happened, what he had done. He found himself walking in the opposite direction of the spring, along the Waterloo Road.

He didn't know what he would do next, but he knew he wouldn't return to that house. His uncle would be only too glad to beat him with a stick or to whip him with his leather belt. And worse would be Joe, who was older and bigger and stronger and, with the unspoken consent accorded by his parents' anger, would beat him further with his fists.

Malachy walked in the cold air, past the crossroad leading to the bridge, past the general store, past the post office. A few minutes after he passed the feed mill, he was aware of a team coming up behind him. He saw two big Belgians, a man with a kindly face bundled under a buffalo robe, a sled loaded with bags of feed. As the sled passed him, he ran after it and clambered on.

This was a common enough game that lots of children played, to hitch a ride on a sleigh or a wagon for a few hundred yards.

He had been seen by the man, or perhaps the man had noticed the extra weight on his sled. He turned from where he was and gave Malachy a small smile as if to say, I know the game and played it myself when I was young. The man turned his attention back to the road and his horses. Malachy, at the back of the sled, made himself comfortable among the bags of feed and, like the man, looked at the road ahead.

They'd gone a good mile when the man turned back to Malachy and asked, "Where are you going?"

"I'm going with you," said Malachy.

"Yes," said the man who understood a joke when he heard one, "but, where are you going?"

"I'm going with you," repeated Malachy, who wasn't joking at all.

The man looked at Malachy for a long moment, unsure what to do. The horses kept up their steady gait and another mile passed and then another and another after that and when they got to the man's barn and unhitched the horses and unloaded the bags of feed and met the man's wife, it was dinner time. Malachy stayed for dinner and for supper and then for the night.

In the end, he stayed with the man and his wife until they grew old and passed away and Malachy continued on with the farm and met a young woman and raised a family and saw his grandchildren born.

And, if he had lived a little longer, he might also have seen me, for Malachy was my great grandfather. I don't know how much of this story is true but it's been with me a long time and, like my name, was handed down to me as I now hand it on to you.

The Golden Hawk

Just after he went around Halverson's corner, Jimmy tried again.

It was a good place to try. The road was almost flat and there was a lot of hard pack, where passing traffic had left a smooth, solid, almost oily surface. It wasn't exactly like the asphalt pavement the town kids could ride on, but it was almost as good. Jimmy didn't want to be going too fast, but he couldn't go too slowly either because if he went too slowly the front wheel would wobble. That was another thing. He didn't have a store-bought bike like the town kids had.

As he pedalled just a little faster, Jimmy took his left hand off the handlebar. He aimed for a patch of hard pack and, as he came to it, he lifted his right hand in the air.

Almost immediately the bike started to wobble. Both of Jimmy's hands fell back onto the handlebars. He would try again going faster. He leaned forward with his head down and lifted himself off the seat. He pumped hard with his legs, using his whole body to push down, first on one pedal, then the other. He loved the feeling of acceleration. For a moment, he stared at the blur of road below his churning legs. Then he eased up, returned to a sitting position and lifted his head to scan the road for the next good patch.

That was when he saw the bird.

It was a bird Jimmy had never before seen, but he knew right away it was a hawk. It was so close that Jimmy, for a moment, had the sensation that he might have reached out his hand and snatched the bird in mid-flight. It was moving that slowly and that low to the ground. For a second, the bird seemed to falter, to dip, and then, with an effort that Jimmy could feel, its wings lifted it above the hay growing tall in Halverson's field. Jimmy came to a quick and quiet stop without ever taking his eyes off the bird. Its underbelly was almost white, but its wings and back were darker. It was a young bird; Jimmy couldn't have explained how he knew that, but he was sure of it. As the hawk continued to gain altitude, its wings seemed to lift and fall with growing confidence and with less and less effort. Then, all of a sudden, the wings stopped beating. They remained effortlessly outstretched. They teetered one way, then tottered the other, as if the hawk was trying to keep its balance on an invisible beam. As he watched, Jimmy could see that the bird was rising, tilting its wings to lean into a curve, and rising yet higher. Jimmy was completely captivated.

"…off the road, ya stupid kid!"

With the words and overwhelming noise came a gust of wind so strong that it pushed Jimmy off balance. At the same instant, he was in the middle of a cloud of dust that made him close his eyes. Too late, he snapped his mouth shut and tasted the bitter dryness of gravel on his tongue. He coughed and spat as he tried to regain his balance. He moved his foot to try to stay standing. His schoolbag shifted its weight. He leaned. He put out his arm. The schoolbag shifted more. He moved his foot again. This time his leg hit the crossbar. He tried to hold his balance….

…. Jimmy found himself on the ground, entangled with his bicycle and his schoolbag. It was hard for Jimmy not to cry. The truck, because that was what had roared by him and knocked him over, had scared him. Now he was half pinned under his own bike and it felt as if he couldn't move. He knew that he had scraped his left knee. He had felt the same kind of pain more than once. He could imagine the skin scraped off, the blood welling to the surface and starting to flow. Jimmy didn't want to look at his knee, nor did he want to look at the heel of his left hand, because it too felt as if it had been scraped.

It took forever to liberate the schoolbag from his shoulders and then get himself disentangled from the bike. All the time, he kept spitting out sand and grit. He found a cut on his right hand, a small, straight line as thin and red as if Miss Rousseau had underlined one of his spelling mistakes. It was strange because even though it was unmistakably a fresh cut, Jimmy didn't feel the least bit of pain. When Jimmy looked at the heel of his left hand, which was now starting to burn, he saw that he had scraped off a few layers of skin. There were shades of white and unexpected pink, speckled with small, sharp, imbedded stones, which he tried to gently brush off. Only then did he dare look at his knee.

"Oh, no!"

Jimmy was looking down at his knee, but it wasn't his knee that made him cry out. It was his pants. He knew his mother was going to be upset. This was his last pair of school pants, the last pair that didn't have a patch or traces of mending. They were pants that were only just a little too big, that were meant to last him at least to the start of the next school year. And he hated the thought of what could happen at school when he had a tear in his clothes. Someone would see it and then they'd pick at it. Jeremy and Randy and Lloyd. They'd laugh at him and then they'd try to tear the hole bigger. They'd make his day miserable in any way they could. He wished he could just go home and not go to school.

School! He was going to be late for school!

"Straight to school now. No dillydallying!" That's what Jimmy's mom had told him when she had found him in the garage that morning.

Jimmy had gone to the garage to say bye to his dad. His dad was just going into the pit to change the oil on Mr. Tremblay's brand new Studebaker. Jimmy had squatted down to say bye, and to look again at the car. Studebakers were Jimmy's favourite cars. He liked Mr. Tremblay's Studebaker well enough, but Jimmy knew that when he was big, he was going to have a different Studebaker. He was going to have a Golden Hawk. He liked to study Mr. Tremblay's car just the same. He liked to see the car from underneath. His dad was just removing the plug from the oil pan, ready to catch the gush of dark, thick liquid that was about to spill out. Then suddenly, there had been his mom, yelling at him that he was going to be late.

Now, he really was going to be late.

JIMMY SCRAMBLED TO HIS FEET. He reached down and grabbed his scuffed school bag off the gravel. He settled it as comfortably as he could on his shoulders and reached down for the handlebars of his bike. Jimmy was small for his age and the bike was big and heavy. Still, Jimmy had learned how to do this and in one quick motion lifted it, pushed off with his right foot and began to swing his leg over the crossbar. Even before he could complete this well-practiced motion, Jimmy knew something was wrong. He was off balance. Jimmy was able to push himself away, so the bike didn't fall on him, but, for the second time that morning, Jimmy found himself sprawled on the gravel road.

This time, he couldn't help it. He cried.

Jimmy cried until he realized that he was sitting in the middle of the road, crying. He wiped his eyes with his shirtsleeves. He ignored the heel of his left hand which felt as if it were on fire. He picked up his schoolbag and carried it to the side of the road and dropped it in the tall grass. Then he went back and picked up the bike by the handlebars and walked it to the side of the road. Jimmy looked at the big sprocket to see what had caused the bike to stop so suddenly. There wasn't anything he could see. There didn't seem to be anything on the small sprocket either. Careful not to get himself or his clothes dirty, Jimmy held the bike by the seat with his left hand and turned the pedal with his right. It took a strong push but, once started, the pedal moved fluidly through its circle. When he stopped pushing and turned the pedal in the opposite direction, the chain caught and immediately stopped the free-spinning rear wheel. The bike seemed to be working.

Jimmy rode the rest of the way to school with both hands on the handlebars. His mind was taken up worrying about how late he would be. He knew he would have to report to the Office. He hoped it would just be Miss Anderchuck. He hoped Mr. Massini wouldn't be there, or better yet, if he could be in his office at the back with his door closed. Miss Anderchuck would give you a note and smile at you, but Mr. Massini would ask you questions and say things and sometimes he even yelled at you, even if it wasn't your fault that you were late. Jimmy rode his bike into an empty and quiet schoolyard feeling very hollow inside.

The big wood door felt heavier than usual and the corridor seemed like a silent, scary tunnel. Jimmy was conscious of every footstep, of every squeak of his soles on the hard, tiled floor. He was just a few steps away from the Office when Miss Weyburn stepped into the corridor. She was reading a paper that she was holding in her hand but looked up and started to smile at Jimmy, but her face suddenly changed.

"What happened to you? You fell off your bike, didn't you? Come into the clinic and we'll get those scrapes looked after and get you cleaned up. Where did this happen?"

Jimmy stepped into the small room next to the Office, which was Nurse Weyburn's clinic on those days that she was in the school. He told her about the truck and falling off the bike. He was surprised when she wiped his face with a cloth and then showed him a large, dark smudge of grease. He sat perfectly still, even when she cleaned his cuts and put iodine on them. With gauze and white tape, she bandaged his knee and his hand. Best of all, she pinned the tear in his pants so it almost didn't show.

It was Nurse Weyburn who went into the Office to get his late slip—Jimmy gladly waited in the hall—and it was Nurse Weyburn who knocked at his classroom door and, in the hall, quietly spoke to Miss Rousseau while he put his school bag in his locker. Both Nurse Weyburn and Miss Rousseau smiled at him as he said, "Excuse me," and slipped past them into the classroom.

Buoyed by the warmth of their smiles Jimmy floated into the classroom. He was aware that almost everyone was looking at him. Usually, knowing someone was looking at him made Jimmy uncomfortable and he would raise his shoulders and bring his head down and turn as if he had to urgently look at something on his left elbow. This time, without knowing why, Jimmy kept his head up. He tried to avoid looking at anybody; he focused on the board at the back of the room.

"Hey, Dork!"

Before he could look down, Jimmy's left leg tripped over something in the aisle. For the third time that morning, Jimmy found himself falling. This time, though, it was different. It was as if, before gravity took hold of him, he had been given a minute to prepare. In that minute, he knew that it was Ron who had tripped him. He could see that he was falling towards his left and that his left hand was the one that was already reaching out to break his fall. He realized that he must protect his left hand. Without knowing how, Jimmy fell on his forearm, with his left hand tucked close to his body. His books clattered to the floor.

"What's going on?" Miss Rousseau was back in the classroom. Jimmy, half on the floor and scrambling to get up, couldn't see her, but he felt the bite of her words. Jimmy knew he had to get to his feet and say something to Miss Rousseau, but he felt as if he were moving under water. Everything was so slow and so silent.

Then someone beside him was standing. It was Mary-Jo Bolentik.

"Jimmy dropped his books, Miss Rousseau," said Mary-Jo. Then, as everyone—including Jimmy—watched, Mary-Jo picked up Jimmy's reader and handed it to him.

An hour later, the recess bell rang. The children rose and stood beside their desks as Miss Rousseau released them row by row. Jimmy's row was the last to be dismissed. As Jimmy neared the door, he heard Miss Rousseau's voice.

"Jimmy, could I see you before you go out? Just close the door a minute, please Mary-Jo."

"Jimmy," began Miss Rousseau, and then she paused so long that Jimmy finally said something.

"Yes, Miss Rousseau," he said.

"Jimmy," repeated Miss Rousseau, and she paused again. Then, just as Jimmy was getting ready to repeat his words, his teacher turned to him and asked him the strangest question.

"Jimmy, are you good friends with Mary-Jo Bolentik?"

Jimmy should have answered no. He hardly ever spoke to her. But he was so surprised by the question that he said nothing at all. As he stood in front of Miss Rousseau, he remembered the way Mary-Jo Bolentik had picked up his books and given them to him. He remembered the way she had spoken up and covered for him. Jimmy stared at Miss Rousseau and felt an unfamiliar wave of warmth wash up his neck and to his cheeks. He couldn't see them, but his ears felt as if they were burning.

"I'm sorry," said Miss Rousseau. She looked down for a second and then, her voice suddenly brisk and business-like, said, "Jimmy, how do you think you did on Monday's math test?"

This was a question Jimmy could answer even though it took him a minute to find his tongue. "I think I did ok."

"Most children find fractions a little difficult at first. Do you find fractions hard?"

"Fractions are ok," replied Jimmy.

"Can I ask you a few questions right now? Can you simplify twelve sixteenths?"

"That's…," said Jimmy. "That's three quarters."

"Can you add two eighths and three eighths?"

"That's….five eighths," said Jimmy.

"What's seven twelfths minus one half?"

"That's one half...that's six twelfths...that's one twelfth," said Jimmy.

"Very good, Jimmy," said Miss Rousseau. "Thank you. Run outside and enjoy the rest of your recess."

Jimmy felt puzzled and, for a second, he looked at Miss Rousseau. She returned his gaze and gave him a smile that seemed to say, "Everything is fine with the world."

Jimmy didn't mind that, for him, it would be a shortened recess. For one thing, he couldn't bend his left knee very much, not without feeling pain. He walked with a stiff leg, almost like Long John Silver would walk. Even before he got to the playground, he knew he wouldn't be able to do much more than stand around. He went out into the sunlight and wandered just a few yards beyond the door. He looked out over the playground and saw it the way Mr. Massini would see it: lots and lots of children, running, walking, playing. Jimmy saw that he wasn't the only one standing around. He saw Ron standing with Jeremy, Randy and Lloyd in a tight little circle, near the gate, away from the others.

After recess, it was math and Miss Rousseau started by talking about yesterday's test. "Overall, we didn't do quite as well as we usually do," she said. "Come to the front to get your paper when I call your name."

As often happened, Mary-Jo's name was called first. Sometimes Pamela or Audrey or Jeffrey Winters might score higher, but it was usually Mary-Jo who got the highest marks in the class. The big surprise was the second name that Miss Rousseau called—Jimmy. It took Jimmy a long minute to get out of his seat and walk to the front. In part, it was the surprise of hearing his name called so soon, but it was something else as well. Jimmy's brain was trying to tell him something and Jimmy couldn't make out what it was. It was a little like being in a dream.

"Well done, Jimmy," said Miss Rousseau with a big smile. "I'm very proud of you."

Jimmy almost forgot to say thank you. He turned and, as he had earlier that morning, he kept his head up. He looked over the heads of his classmates towards the board at the back of the room. As he took one step after the other, even his knee seemed to feel better. He let his eyes drop just a bit, and saw the faces of his classmates. Some turned towards him, others not. And he saw something else. He saw Ron, looking towards the corner where Lloyd and Jeremy sat, and they were looking back at Ron, nodding yes.

Jimmy was suddenly alert. He held his math paper firmly in his right hand and walked gingerly back towards his seat. He kept his head up and avoided eye contact with anybody, and especially with Ron. He made a show of not looking directly where he was going, but his peripheral vision was firmly focused on the narrow aisle leading to his desk. He wasn't at all surprised that Ron's foot was suddenly sticking out into the aisle to trip him. Jimmy, in a way that he hoped looked accidental, took a half hop on his left leg and then, with his right foot turned outward as if to kick a soccer ball, he kicked Ron's ankle as hard as the narrow space permitted.

Even as Ron cried out, as much in surprise as in pain, Jimmy moved quickly out of the way of any retaliatory action.

"What's going on?" called Miss Rousseau.

His head high, and speaking louder than he normally did, Jimmy said, "Excuse me. I almost tripped."

Miss Rousseau stared at them for a long few seconds, but Jimmy knew her anger was not directed at him.

As he turned to walk the last few steps to his desk, his eyes met Mary-Jo's. Her eyes were more grey than blue, a colour Jimmy couldn't name, and they were looking straight at him. What happened next, happened in a fraction of a second. Even as Jimmy looked straight into her eyes, he saw them change. They began to sparkle. They seemed to be full of light. Jimmy had time to see that Mary-Jo's whole face was smiling at him. He couldn't be sure but, as he sat down, he thought he heard her say, "Good for you, Jimmy."

He sat and looked at his paper. He didn't want to look at the corner where Lloyd and Jeremy sat. They would raise their fists at him, a threat they'd try to make good on at lunch time. He looked at his paper and pretended to study it. But he wasn't seeing fractions written out in pencil or the small, neat check marks ticked down the page in red ink. He looked at his paper and saw a bird that was both menacing and beautiful. A bird with dark eyes and a sharp, hooked beak. Its wings moved laboriously and looked both fragile and frighteningly strong. It had a white belly and a dark back and Jimmy saw it clear the stretching spears of timothy and rise higher and higher into a bright, cloudless sky.

Sugden

I closed the book and, my back and thighs sore from sitting, I struggled slowly to my feet, and shuffled like a two-year old to the window. The picture window is triple-glazed but standing so close, I could feel cold radiating from it. Under my bathrobe, I was bundled in three layers including what I think of as my track suit, which despite its age and ragged appearance, is the most comfortable and warmest thing I own. What had the thermometer outside the kitchen window read this morning? Minus fifteen? But that was a protected corner on the lee side of the house. It looked much colder.

The wind off the lake appeared to be picking up. The snow was easing off, no longer falling as thickly as it had through the night and early morning when it came down in heavy flakes. Now gusts were causing it to swirl, almost like small white tornados that would momentarily materialize and then subside, leaving the flakes to fall into slowly growing drifts. It was hard to tell how much snow had actually fallen since last night. The bird feeder, which had stood empty since the accident, was at least three quarters buried in snow, but in the far corner of the garden, the dry stems of last summer's red phlox seemed little more than ankle-deep in white powder.

Winter had come early this year. Today was the 18th of December and this was already the third storm of the season. Snow had been on the ground since late November.

Looking out, there was nothing to see beyond Nadeau's Point. Earth and sky faded into a uniform white-grey haze. Even the dark water of the lake, beyond the Point, disappeared into the blankness of wind and falling snow. It was as if the entire world extended no further than the few hundred yards beyond the sheet of glass behind which I stood, warm and protected. And, if I were to step outside, I too, within minutes, would disappear.

The phone rang and startled me out of my reverie. I turned and slowly started shuffling towards the front hall, cursing my foolishness for not having brought the portable with me. Four, five, six rings, and then the answering machine clicked on and I heard my voice, my old voice, reciting my number and asking the caller to leave a message. And then, as I lumbered slowly towards it, I heard Peggy speaking, her voice still tinged with a decades-old accent she clings to the way I cling to my track suit.

"Morning, Love. Hope I didn't wake you from a nap. Just called to say we made it back despite the weather. Jack insisted on leaving yesterday, storm or no storm. It was an absolutely horrid drive. Took us almost twelve hours. But we're home. If the snow lets up, I'll bring you some soup later on. I've just got it simmering on the stove top now. We'll talk later. Ta-ta for now."

I heard the machine click off even as my hand touched the phone. I thought that I should call her back right away, but something in me didn't want to. Peggy had been wonderful the last two months. I appreciated her, and the others, the friends and neighbours who'd come to visit and put up with my tears and pampered me with food and gifts. I did appreciate them, but then, at that moment, I didn't want to call Peggy. I wanted to be alone, to have my cocoon to myself.

With more determination and less pain than yesterday, I shuffled on as far as the kitchen and then turned back on my steps. I made the trip four times before I suddenly felt utterly exhausted. I sat in my study, feeling both incredibly proud and hopelessly inadequate. That I could move at all was a wonder, but at the same time I wondered how I would live with such limited movement. I could not imagine venturing beyond the ground floor. Yet, I felt grateful for its comfort. I was home, and grateful to be home. I was no longer tightly confined within the four efficient and sterile walls of a hospital room.

It seemed that almost every action was a strain, that every movement hurt. What was that line? I feel pain, but am glad because it reminds me that I am still alive. Where had I read that?

I eased myself fully into my chair and rested my book on my lap. I looked at it and couldn't decide whether or not I wanted to pick it up. It came from Peggy and I wondered what had prompted her to select this particular book for me. It is the story of Albert Johnson, the mad trapper of Rat River, a man whose origins are not entirely clear, whose motives are even less certain, and whose death seems to me as pointless and violent as it was costly.

What was the line about the North being too fragile to be the refuge of civilization's most dangerous and unwanted elements? Had I just read that in these pages, or had it come from somewhere else? I wondered again if the accident had taken my memory as well as my mobility.

I left the book closed on my lap and I looked towards the window. On the other side, the wind was swirling the snow with careless vigour and energy. Dandurand's red-roofed cabin which even in the summer peeks through the foliage on Nadeau's Point was invisible, erased by the grey-white powdery cloud that seemed to be closing in on me.

I picked up the book and, not up to the effort of reading, let it fall open to the half dozen pages of photographs. I had looked at these already several times. The RCMP officers who had hunted him down; Wop May, the bush pilot who had been instrumental in finding him; Johnson himself, grimacing in death, transformed by the camera's lens into something more like a werewolf than a human being. And then, in another photo, a face that couldn't possibly have been, but looked so much like another face.

છ

I was twelve the summer we moved to Montrouge. We'd celebrated my birthday at Nan's and two days later we'd left in the station wagon, following the big orange moving van that was carting everything from our Montreal apartment to our new home in Montrouge. Mom drove, at least she drove from Montreal to the other side of Quebec City and then she relented and let Michael drive. Michael had turned sixteen a few months earlier and had earned his driver's license almost the next day. That was possible in those days when driver's ed was for newly-widowed, middle-aged women learning to do the tasks their husbands had always done. Today, everyone has to take driver's ed. Strange to think that the eighteen-year-old who crashed into us would have also taken driver's ed.

I think it was Michael who drove the rest of the way to Sept-Îles, where Dad met us. Dad had been in Montrouge for the better part of the previous year. In the spring Mom had left Michael and me with Nan to make the trip north to help Dad choose a house. I think that had been one of the conditions that Mom had set, that and a five-year limit. Looking back, I can understand, as I didn't then, how hard a decision it was for both of them. Nan, although I didn't know it, was already not well, and Mom must have felt bad about leaving. For Dad, it was an opportunity he felt he couldn't afford to ignore; a last chance, as he put it, to make real money. I had caught bits and pieces of their conversations in the weeks before Dad went north, conversations that grew loud and then soft, that were sometimes interrupted by a sound I had never really heard, that of Mom crying.

Dad met us in Sept-Îles and the next day we boarded a train that took us through forests and up river valleys, and through unexpected tunnels and, a couple of times, made us feel as though we were in mid-air because we'd look out the window and look down on tree tops. It was scary, and yet, I loved that train ride. I ended up taking it several times over the next five years and it never ceased to impress me and move me. I think I liked Montrouge from the moment we got there just because the ride up had been so spectacular.

We spent our first night in the hotel and the next day Dad drove us around. First, he drove by what was going to be our home and then he drove through the rest of the town. He showed us the men's quarters where he had been staying until now, the English school, which Michael and I would be attending, the much bigger French school, the arena, the pool, the strip mall which, Dad told us, was built to act as a windbreak for the town. Dad drove down the road that led to the open pit mine and the hangar where he worked on the giant Terex trucks that hauled the iron ore out of the mine. By the time we got back to Montrouge, the moving van had arrived at our house and was already half unloaded.

Thinking back on it, Montrouge was an almost unreal place. It was a modern suburb in the middle of wilderness, surrounded by mountains and forests and ice-cold lakes. Today, of course, it's even more unreal. I saw photos of it on the Internet a while ago and there is nothing left. After the mine closed, all the buildings were bulldozed to rubble and buried. All that's left is a surreal network of streets and sidewalks slowly being reclaimed by vegetation.

But for the five years we spent there, it was a fabulous place. I remember, even before we got unpacked, neighbours came over with coffee cakes and casseroles to welcome us. I met Annie and Marion the first day there and we remained best friends right through high school.

It was late August when we got to Montrouge, but in those ten or twelve days before school started, I became an old-timer. With Annie and Marion and three or four others, I explored the town from end to end. And we went far beyond the town. We'd go to the lake and stand on the white beach and skip stones, or roll up our pant legs and stand shin-deep in water until our feet turned blue with cold to see who could suffer the longest. We'd haul our fathers' tools and scavenged lumber into the woods and try to build tree forts. We'd walk out to the dump and throw small rocks at the black bears and sometimes do as the bears did and go through the dump ourselves and marvel at some of the treasures we found.

When school started, it was as much of a wondrous revelation as the town itself had been. I was starting my first year of high school. Back in Montreal, I would have been packed like a sardine with thirty-five other kids into a cramped and dusty old classroom. Not so in Montrouge! It was a small school but, like the rest of the town, it was new. There might have been a hundred kids in all, from kindergarten to Grade 11. Besides Annie and me (Marion was a year ahead of us), there were only four others in my class: Rebecca, Chris, Andrew and Stephen. I was one of those kids who, until I'd arrived at Montrouge and discovered the joys of being a tomboy, had always been a bookworm. I had always liked school, and I had always done well. It was the same at Montrouge, but more so. It was so much more relaxed, almost as if we were attending some posh private school, or as if we were being educated by private tutors.

I remember some wonderful teachers. My favourite, or at least one of my favourites, my first favourite, was Mrs. Williams who taught us English and History the first three years. I adored her. For one thing, at that time I was convinced that I was going to become a writer and illustrator of children's books. I remember sharing my first book with her. It was the story of a toad named Terrance who lived under a bush near a pond. I struggled desperately to illustrate the story and the more I worked at it, the worse my drawings became. But she encouraged me, with the illustrating as well as with the writing.

Mrs. Williams was a kindred spirit. I didn't learn it until just before she left at the end of Grade 9, but she too was working at becoming a writer. She wrote poetry and it was only at the very end of that last school year that she told us. She read us a few of her poems the last day of school and we listened, or at least, I listened, mesmerized by her voice, because she had a lovely voice, but puzzled and confused by the words. Perhaps it showed on our faces.

Mrs. Williams moved back south and I know I kept waiting to hear that she'd become a famous author, but I never heard anything more about her. I googled her name several years ago and learned that she too had given up on writing, unless perhaps she was pseudonymously self-publishing some of her work. But she did get involved in writing; she had become an editor, with McClelland and Stewart.

It was because Mrs. Williams left that we got Sugden the next year, in Grade 10. I remember that when I walked into the classroom and saw him, I had a sudden visceral reaction to him that I'd never before experienced, and never have since. I literally took a step back, as if I'd come against a grisly sight or been hit by a foul odour. He looked like a slug. He was of medium height, I think, but he seemed to have a shapeless body, as if he were all flesh with no bones. He was balding and he was one of those men who try to hide it by wearing a very low part and combing the hair against the grain and over the bald top. I remember him as grey, a nondescript, washed-out colour. He always wore the same rumpled grey suit and his shirt collar always looked as if it needed washing and his tie always looked tattered and stained. I knew he lived in the men's quarters so I supposed he had no one to care for his clothes and he had never learned himself.

Perhaps because of Mrs. Williams or perhaps because of my childhood aspirations, until then English had been my favourite subject. I had always loved to read and language had started to intrigue me, fascinate me. And of course, I wanted to write.

Within a month, I dreaded both English and History. Sugden would hand out a new book—I can't even remember a single title from Grade 10, although I could probably name every single book I did with Mrs. Williams—and open it up and start reading to us. What killed it was that he was a poor reader. He would stumble over words or mispronounce them. He would get half way through a sentence and realize that he'd misread it and go back and start it over and get it wrong the second time as well. And he had a slightly nasal voice that grated on my nerves. He was one of those teachers who gave dull assignments—How I Spent My Summer Vacation—and returned your paper with a mark at the end, but not a single comment, as if he had done no more than write an arbitrary number in red ink.

When I got back my first assignment with him, I couldn't believe he'd given me 73 out of 100, because for the last three years with Mrs. Williams my marks were always in the high eighties and low nineties.

"Go and see him," Annie told me. Unlike me, Annie was a fighter. She was small and slim with dark hair and freckles. She looked angelic but she was one of the toughest people I have ever met. I never saw her back down from anyone.

"Sir, I don't understand this mark."

"That's 73 percent."

"Yes, but I don't understand how I got it."

"Oh, I see. Well, there were things about your paper that were good. Parts of it were probably quite good, but it wasn't consistent. The writing sometimes was a little weak. I think you might have worked on it a little more."

I didn't know what to say. Then I felt Annie's fist smash into the small of my back.

"It's just that I usually get better marks."

"Well," Sugden gave a false laugh, "maybe sometimes I mark a little hard. But it's for your own good. It's important to go over your work. Revise it. Re-read it. You can always improve on it."

"Mikaela always gets the highest marks in the class." It was Annie who had decided to step in. After three years with her,

I knew a lot of things about Annie and I recognized the tone in her voice. It had an edge. It was a warning.

"Yes, well, this is Grade 10 and..." Sugden began.

"That's not a very good mark."

I turned towards Annie. I was now afraid of what she might say, or what she might do. Her face was set and her eyes were brimming with defiance. Sugden must have seen what I did because he backed down.

"Why don't you leave your paper with me," he said, "and I'll take a second look at it tonight."

The next day he gave it back to me without a word. The 73% had been crossed out and underneath it he had written, in smaller script, 90%. For the rest of the year, regardless of what I handed in, whether I slaved over an assignment or tossed it off without a thought, I always got 90.

We were a small group, as I said—even smaller because Rachel had moved back south—and we had been together for the last three years. By the time we got back our fourth assignment, we were aware that we were always getting the same mark, and that mark was exactly the same as our Grade 9 year's average.

Except for Chris. Chris's marks in English had jumped twenty percent and he was suddenly scoring as high as I was. We had teased him about it the first few times, but we saw that it bothered him, much more than it might have bothered us. And we realized that there wasn't anything he could do about it.

Chris was one of us, but perhaps the one who was the closest to being an outsider. He was a very good-looking boy, and my first crush. It was in Grade 9 that I had first started noticing boys and Chris was the first boy I noticed. For two months I had gone to bed with images of Chris in my head: his longish blonde hair that half fell over the left side of his face, his blue eyes, and his mouth; Chris had a soft, sensuous mouth with lips that were slightly puffy and pink, almost as if he were wearing a very faint lipstick. I'd fall asleep wondering what it would be like to kiss his lips. He was tall and I think he was self conscious about it because he was always a little stooped. I think his height appealed to me because that had been the summer that I had suddenly shot up so that I was almost as tall as Michael when he came back from his first year at University.

Chris was perhaps a little quieter than the rest of us. He didn't go in much for sports, and in Montrouge sports was the biggest thing in town. While all the boys played hockey, Chris, for a short while, had tried to take up figure skating. He was razzed for it, of course, and perhaps that's what had made him give it up. Or perhaps he didn't have the skill. He would have been very tall for a figure skater. And he was artsy. He drew amazingly well and in Grade 8, when Mrs. Williams had introduced us to water colours, she had ended up framing four of his paintings and they had hung for a month in the foyer of the town library as part of an exhibition. I was more than a little jealous of his talent but I never had the courage to ask him to make a drawing to go with one of my stories.

It didn't take us long to see that Chris was Sugden's pet. Kids are sensitive to that sort of thing. The unusually high marks that Chris got were part of it, but there were all the other things that, taken individually, meant nothing, but when you added them all up, they left you with an inescapable conclusion. Maybe I was the most conscious of it, and, if I hadn't found Sugden such a disgusting creature, maybe it would have upset me, or left me jealous. I felt a tinge of that anyway, just because, for the last three years, and even though she showed it much less than Sugden, I had been the favourite in English class, I had been Mrs. Williams's pet.

At first, Chris had seemed ok with being the teacher's pet, had perhaps even relished his new position at the head of the class, as it were. Nobody, including Chris, could explain it, but we had lots of other things to think about and with each passing week, for me at least, English and History classes grew less and less important. Then, something happened. I don't know what, but something definitely happened. We walked into English class one morning and it was all different. Where Chris had been friendly and co-operative with Sugden, he suddenly became curt, surly, hostile. And, unusual for him, because he was a caring and sensitive person by nature and would suffer himself rather than hurt someone's feelings, he started openly showing his dislike, his disdain for Sugden. We all hated Sugden, but Chris was the only one who didn't bother to hide it.

What was strange was that Sugden didn't react in any way to Chris's sudden change. He continued treating Chris like his pet, continued giving him high marks. It was strange. But then, everything about Sugden was strange. His English classes, like I said, were deadly dull. If he didn't spend the class putting us to sleep with his stumbling monotone, he would give us what he called "work time" during which we were supposed to work on whatever it was that we wanted to work on, and I'd spend the period doodling or chatting with Annie. His History class, if anything, was worse. Regardless of what we were supposed to be reading or studying, he always ended up talking about death and torture. He'd tell us how a thumbscrew worked, or take a whole period to describe what drawing and quartering was, or explain how someone who was burned at the stake would die of smoke inhalation before the fire could really burn him.

As it turned out, Sugden's bland equanimity in the face of Chris's insolence was just a front, and Sugden was a lot sicker than any of us ever guessed.

Because he was the English teacher, Sugden was in charge of the school play, just as Mrs. Williams had been previously. Looking back, it made perfect sense that Sugden would have picked the play he did, a murder mystery entitled *I'll Be Back Before Midnight*, which, among other things, called for one of the characters to appear very briefly on the stage hanging like a dead man on the end of a noose.

The annual school play was a big deal, almost as big as basketball and soccer. All the high school kids got involved and the play was always put on at the community center which had an auditorium with a really well-equipped theatre. And it wasn't just the kids who got involved; it was the parents as well. The mothers sewed costumes and the fathers showed off their carpentry skills. My dad, because he was now in charge of the garage at the mine and had to look after hydraulic systems on the trucks and all the other machinery, was in particular demand. The year before, Mrs. Williams had mounted *A Man for All Seasons* and Dad had designed and built a platform that not only rose three feet off the stage, but rotated a hundred and eighty degrees as well.

On this play, it had fallen to Dad to come up with a way to make sure that the student left hanging at the end of a noose would be alive and well and back in class on Monday morning. What Dad came up with was a marvel of simplicity: a body harness which the actor would wear under his costume and which would be attached by a length of black electrical cord to a pulley mechanism back stage. The actor would have to let his body relax and his head fall to one side to simulate a hanged man. Throughout the scene, which would last just long enough to make the audience gasp in shock and horror, his weight would be supported by the harness and the electrical cord.

I remember at supper one night telling Dad that we could probably do the scene even without the harness. "A man who is hung doesn't choke to death," I said, brimming with Sugden's macabre store of knowledge. "It's a slip knot and all, but when you get sentenced to hang to death, it's really that your neck gets broken when you go through the trap door. It's the fall that breaks your neck and kills you."

"Maybe," Dad replied, "but why take chances?"

It didn't come as much of a surprise to any of us that Chris was cast in the part of the character who gets hung, although one of the boys in Grade 11 was pretty upset about it. It was something of an unwritten rule that the kids in Grade 11 had seniority when it came to auditioning for parts. After all, they were graduating and this would be their last chance to go on stage. The role of the dead man was the choicest part in the play. As kids, we'd grown up playing cops and robbers, and each of us would have loved to do a death scene on a real stage.

The school play was always put on toward the end of March and the two weeks before were always very intense. Twice-weekly rehearsals which had been going on since January became daily and they shifted from the school to the auditorium. Normally, the kids who were acting in the play would go home after school, grab a quick supper, rest for a short while and then get to the community center for rehearsals which ran from six till nine. The tech crew ran a different schedule; they would go to the auditorium after school and work on the lighting and sets until we arrived, at which point they would head off.

Sometimes a couple of the mothers would come by and ask to see what a costume looked like under the lights and so we'd rehearse a scene with one or two people in costume. Other times one or two of the fathers might also be there for a while to finish up some prop or part of the set. Normally, though, by the end of the evening, it was just the actors and prompters who were still around, and of course the director, who was Sugden.

The first incident, which, initially, almost everyone took to be a freak accident, must have been the week before opening night. (The school play always ran for two nights, so we had opening night, which was always on a Friday, and closing night, on Saturday, and it wasn't uncommon for a good part of the audience to come to both nights.)

We had a rehearsal schedule and we worked on only certain scenes on any given evening until the last week. Then, the Tuesday before the play, we would have the dress rehearsal, which meant doing the entire play in costume. On Wednesday, we'd have the technical rehearsal followed by the full dress rehearsal on Thursday and then opening night on Friday.

There weren't many of us around and it was the end of the evening, almost time to finish up and go home. We'd gone over our scenes long enough that we were starting to forget lines that we knew, just because we were tired. Even though it wasn't scheduled for that night, Sugden suddenly announced that, since we had a few minutes left, that we could try the hanging scene.

We'd done it a few times already, always with my Dad there controlling the pulley. As Chris dug out the harness and put it on, the rest of us started getting our coats and hats and—the scene no longer being a novelty for us—a few of the kids headed out the door. I was still there, and I remember that two of the Grade 11 kids, Samantha and Richard, were still there. They had recently become an item and for them, more than anything, it was an excuse to engage in a bit of quick necking at the back of the auditorium. I stayed because, even though I no longer had a crush on Chris, I enjoyed his company and he lived three doors down from our place. Besides, it was always nicer to walk home with someone than all alone.

Chris got himself all set and, from backstage, Sugden, called out, "Quiet on the set. Go."

Right away, I knew something was wrong. Chris's head wasn't lolling to one side and his body wasn't hanging limp. His neck and head were stretched straight back. His legs were kicking and with his hands he was clutching at the noose around his neck. He was making gurgling sounds, which as a dead man, he wasn't supposed to be making. He was all alone on stage—although that was the way the scene was supposed to be.

I was seven or eight rows back from the stage, right in the middle. I jumped up and as quickly as I could, I rushed towards the aisle so I could get to the stage. All the time I kept yelling, "Mr. Sugden! Mr. Sugden!" Chris was still all alone and struggling like a fish at the end of a line. I couldn't understand where Sugden was. As I ran down the aisle, I turned my head back to yell at Richard and Samantha and I could see that Richard was already scampering down the aisle. I got to the stage and scrambled up and, without knowing what I was doing, I grabbed Chris around the legs and lifted him as best I could. He was heavier than I expected and, with my head crushed against his knees, I couldn't see anything, but I could feel that he wasn't struggling any more. Then Richard was there, lifting him and Chris seemed suddenly to weigh nothing at all. Chris disentangled the noose from his neck and we lowered him to the floor.

"Someone tampered with it," was the first thing Dad said when, later that night, I told him what had happened.

The next night, with everyone there—the stage crew, the actors, even some of the parents, the principal talked about the importance of safety and avoiding accidents. He praised Chris for his commitment to stay with the play, and he thanked Richard and me for acting quickly. He didn't mention Sugden, and he didn't speak for more than two minutes, but everybody knew that he was really talking to only one person.

It was at home that the incident clearly changed from an accident to something else. Dad was angry about it. He had gone to look at the mechanism and, as he had first said, it had been tampered with. The electric cable—chosen because, being black, would be invisible to the audience, and because the wound copper wires would be able to support ten times Chris's weight—had been loosened from the counterweight that acted as a safety. And, Dad kept asking me at the dinner table, where had Sugden been? Why had he not held the cable as he surely knew had to be done if Chris was hanging from the other end?

I felt exactly the same way that Dad did, and we were far from alone.

There were always lots of people around the next week. Dad got a chair and a flashlight and a book and he parked himself backstage next to his pulley mechanism. Chris was always backstage just before the hanging scene and he would cue dad for his few seconds of work and then Dad would go back to reading his book by flashlight. Dad was pretty big and just by sitting there he made it clear that nobody was going to touch anything. But he wasn't the only parent who had assigned himself to guard duty. The three mothers who'd worked on costumes were also there, in the front row, every single evening. Chris's dad, who'd helped out with the sets, was also there every night. He was tall, like his son, and he was one of those people who have a hard time sitting still. He kept wandering backstage, asking if he could help out with one thing or another. By that time, of course, the best thing he could do was stay out of the way. Finally, one of the mothers managed to tell him that. He would sit next to the three mothers in the front row, fidgety and inattentive.

Given the number of adults who were constantly around, what happened on Thursday night is almost unbelievable. This was dress rehearsal and everybody was pretty wound up. The actors had clear instructions. We had to be at the theatre by five thirty and in costume and make-up by six forty-five. We could hang around the dressing room, or the green room, but every place else was strictly out of bounds, especially the stage. The kids who worked stage crew had similar instructions. They would do a sound and light check at six and then patiently wait till seven when one of them would open the curtain and we'd go through the play from top to bottom in front of an almost empty house. Although this year it wouldn't be that empty at all.

None of the actors saw what happened, but we all heard it. Maybe ten or fifteen minutes before curtain there was a tremendous crash on the stage. Rules and instructions not-withstanding, everybody rushed out to see what had hap-pened. We poured onto the stage from the wings and the parents, sitting on the other side of the closed curtains, rushed up from their seats in the house.

A fresnel, which is a big, heavy, stage light, had crashed down from the batten overhead. Nobody was hurt, but there was lots of shattered glass and an ugly gash on the stage floor where the metal frame had dug into the wood.

Dad, who was a foreman and used to giving orders, got us all off the stage. The actors trooped back to the green room and the stage crew went back to their positions. Someone found a janitor who vacuumed up the glass and brought out the stage ladder. Dad got the lighting crew to climb up and check every single fresnel, spotlight and scoop on all three of the battens.

The dress rehearsal was delayed by barely twenty minutes, which, under the circumstances, was pretty amazing. It went badly, which was good because this was the dress rehearsal and, true to form, on Friday and Saturday we brought the house down.

On Sunday morning, Dad went back to being an armchair detective and on Monday morning, two policemen flew in from Quebec City.

There were a couple of strange things about the fresnel which had crashed down. For one thing, there was a forty-foot long piece of nylon fishing line tied to it. Another thing was that the light hadn't been connected to its plug in the batten. Even stranger was that the fresnel wasn't part of the lighting design for the play. Neither Allan nor Teddy, the two kids who had done the lighting, had put the light up and neither remembered seeing it there on Wednesday when we'd done the technical rehearsal. As far as anyone could tell, the light came down when Teddy and Allan, who were goofing around, pulled on some of the teaser curtains which would have brushed against the batten the light was on.

What brought the police was that where it crashed on the stage was the exact spot where Chris would have been standing about a minute into the play.

The two policemen left Montrouge on Tuesday, the day after they arrived. They interviewed lots of people, including Teddy and Allan, and of course, Sugden, but they left without arresting anybody.

As Dad explained it, all the evidence was circumstantial. A spool of nylon fishing line was found in Sugden's desk at school, but there's no law against having a spool of fishing line, even if a desk at school is a strange place to keep it and you're not a fisherman.

Annie's mom, who sat on the school board, explained that the attempt to fire Sugden came to naught because the same day the policemen flew out of Montrouge, the president of the teacher's union flew in. An attempt to fire him wouldn't necessarily be successful, she explained, and, even if it were, it could take months and cost the school board loads of money. The school board would opt to go the bureaucratically safe route, which was to simply decline to renew his contract at the end of the year.

As for us, we banded around Chris like security guards around a VIP. When we walked into Sugden's classes we were a miniature phalanx, with Chris in the middle. In the classroom, we dragged our desks to the back wall and sat behind them like archers behind a battlement. Sugden, who had done precious little teaching anyway, did absolutely none after. He would tell us, "I'll be right back," and not return until the end of the class, just in time to dismiss us. Or, he'd assign us work time and he'd sit at the front pretending to be busy with something while we'd sit at the back and chat or read or catch up on our math homework.

Sugden left Montrouge three days before the end of classes. "He used his sick leave," Annie's mom told us.

Maybe he knew we had spent the last few weeks plotting some sort of good-bye for him. Not that we would ever have turned our plans into reality, and in truth, we hadn't even actually settled on one plan.

Strangely enough, I probably owe a small debt of gratitude to Sugden. He closed a door for me, and true to popular wisdom, another one opened. I gravitated not so much towards Math, but certainly towards Science. In Grade 11, the year after Sugden, I thrived on Physics and Chemistry. My childhood dream of illustrating children's books sublimated like dry ice at room temperature. We left Montrouge three weeks after my graduation and the three of us returned to Montreal. I did a year at Concordia, transferred to Queen's and eventually settled on dentistry, a profession which, all in all, has been remarkably good to me.

℞

I looked again at the photo in the book. The caption described the men as trappers who helped in the RCMP manhunt. Perhaps, somewhere in the text, their names may appear. And what if one of the names was Sugden? What would that tell me?

I looked out at the swirling snow. In the last little while the wind had continued to pick up. I could see even less of the lake than before and its colour seemed to have changed as well. It was less dark now, somehow, as if it too sought to join the earth and sky in a grey-white oblivion.

I had much to worry about. Like the view from my picture window, nothing about my future was very clear. The whirling snow was making me dizzy. I sat back and picked up the book and opened it to my bookmark. I might have the energy to read and, in that case, I might learn something from the death of Albert Johnson.

The Thumb

Gino was awake before his mother's cushioned footsteps entered his room. Like a dark shadow in soft, shuffling slippers she seemed to glide rather than walk over the floor. Through the blankets, he felt her hand's gentle pressure on his shoulder.

"*Gino. Gino. Sono le cinque venti. Svegliati.*"

"Mamma…"

"*Sei già sveglio? Beh, alzati, pigrone. Ha nevicato. C'è pane e marmelata e latte. Dai, alzati.*"

"*Si, Mamma.*"

She removed her hand from his shoulder and slid soundlessly out of the room.

Gino closed his eyes and let out a sigh of disappointment. He had hoped that she would stay. He had hoped that she would sit on the edge of his bed and talk to him for a few minutes. Those were the best mornings, when he could lie still under the covers, with his eyes closed, and listen to his mother's voice pull him gently into wakefulness. It wasn't his mother's actual words that mattered. She might say anything at all. She might tell him what the temperature was that day, or if there was lots of wind, or if it was raining. She might tell him what she was going to make for supper, or that Mr. Bannerman, downstairs, was sick again. It was the sound, and knowing that the sound was just for him. His mother's voice felt different when she spoke just to him, when he wasn't sharing her words with Maria, the baby, or with his sixteen-year-old sister, Graziella. Gino opened his eyes and put his bare feet on the cold linoleum floor.

∾

It was cold enough that Gino could see his breath crystallize. If he exhaled as he passed under a street lamp, he created clouds of small, sharp, multicoloured crystals that momentarily hovered and glittered in mid-air.

His red toque was pulled far down over his forehead and ears. A scarf was wrapped twice around his neck and chin. He wore both his sweaters under his coat and his two thickest pairs of wool socks. Despite all the clothing, when he first left the house, he felt the sharp, frigid needles of cold; his scalp tingled and his nostrils closed. When he inhaled, it felt in his throat like a sip of milk right out of the fridge. He was sure that his skin, under his long johns, was nothing but goose bumps. Now, five minutes later, as he got to the drop off point, he was comfortably warm and hardly aware of the cold.

Three of the bundles had already been picked up and Gino took the smaller of the two that remained. His bundle was marked River Street even though only four of Gino's thirty-eight papers were delivered to River Street. First with bare hands and then, more clumsily, with his mitts on, Gino counted the papers as he stowed them into his two bags. He then folded the heavy brown wrapping paper and tucked it into one of his bags and finally rolled the string into a ball and slipped that into his coat pocket. Today was Wednesday. Next to Saturday, Wednesday's paper was the heaviest of the week. With a practiced motion he heaved the first bag over his left shoulder and then the second over his right shoulder. He shrugged once or twice to make the heavy bags as comfortable as possible before stepping out of the shelter of the loading dock and back onto the street.

He looked west along Cumberland Street, just in case he saw Gary, then turned and began trudging east.

It was going to be a good morning for the papers. There wasn't a wisp of wind. The snow, which had been falling all night, was light and fluffy. It came up over his ankles, but it was easy to walk in. It wasn't at all like the storm on Monday when the snow, more than knee high, had blown into hard drifts that made walking almost impossible. It had taken Gino almost twice as long to do the papers. When he finally got home, as frozen as an icicle, he had to leave again immediately because he was already late for school.

The few minutes it had taken to pick up the papers had been long enough for the cold to make itself felt again. Gino, as much as the newspaper bags would allow, kept his head tucked between his shoulders, turtle-like. He kept his face down so that his red toque cut the cold air. Alone on the sidewalk, he took only occasional upward glances from below his eyebrows. Here, on Cumberland Street, there was hardly a sign of the over-night snowfall. The street and the sidewalk had both been scraped clean. The few cars that passed drove slowly as if still battling Monday's storm. They passed by almost silently, followed by small clouds of exhaust fumes from their mufflers. As he walked, he could hear his footsteps, the brittle sound of boots crunching down on snow crystals.

By the time Gino got to Villa Street, he was, if not warm, at least totally acclimatized and no longer conscious of the cold. Villa Street was where a residential area crossed the storefronts of Cumberland Street. The days he and Gary started their routes together, it was the place where they separated. Gary turned right on Nugent Street while Gino turned north to Court Street and Harrington Avenue to deliver his first seven papers.

The first day Gino had started the paper route, Gary had walked with him as far as Harrington and told him all about delivering papers. Even if you're only delivering three dozen papers, carry them in two bags because it's easier. Mrs. Evans, the dispatcher, is really grumpy but you have to stay on good terms with her because any problems you have, she's the person you have to deal with. It sometimes happens that your bundle is a paper short. You have to call Mrs. Evans as soon as possible and let her know who didn't get the paper. It's always good to have a dime in your pocket. If you have an extra paper, you can throw it away, or keep it. If you're really lucky, you can even sell it. Collection day is Saturday and you really have to keep track of who pays. It's best on Saturday to deliver a little later so that you finish your route at 8:30 or so. Then, you can retrace your steps and collect from your customers. On Saturday you always make sure to start with some change in your pocket because there's always someone too cheap to leave you a fifteen-cent tip. But you have to be nice, even to those people who don't tip, because often they would give you a crisp two-dollar bill, or even a five-dollar bill at Christmas. If you do end up with lots of bills, it's good to keep them in a different pocket, or even better, tucked into your socks. You have to look out for yourself sometimes.

eრე

On Monday, he had had to clamber over shoulder-high snowbanks, but in the two days since the storm, many of the snowbanks had disappeared and some of the sidewalks had been cleared. On College Street too, the snowbanks were gone even though the sidewalk had not been cleared. The street was now silent and empty, but Gino could easily picture it with the snow removal crews. There were always a few men walking in front of, or behind, the key piece of machinery, a giant snowblower. It slowly but systematically chewed its way through any size snowbank, spewing a flurry of ice chunks and snow into the back of a truck to be dumped at the edge of the bay.

Most of Gino's customers had cleaned their walkways of Monday's snowfall. Most, but not all. On Knight Street, at Mrs. Davidson's, Gino negotiated a narrow icy pathway that led to her top step. Her walkway was never cleared and Gino wondered how she got in and out. Mrs. Davidson looked about a hundred years old. Her shoulders were all hunched up and she walked really slowly with a cane. A few of Gino's customers had cleared their walkways but hadn't yet tackled their driveways and their cars sat disguised as smooth, symmetrical drifts of snow.

Gino grew more comfortable as the bags slung over his shoulders grew lighter. Six customers on College Street. Five on Peter. Only two on Elm but eight on Prospect. There was a faint glow of light on the eastern edge of the dark sky as Gino crossed River Street. There were three papers on Elm and four on Peter where those two streets continued north of River Street. At that point he would be down to his last dozen papers. He could then walk back down River Street to Farrand, Wolesley and Ruttan to finish his route. But there was a short cut which was sometimes available to him, and that was to go higher up Peter Street to the unnamed dead-end street that led to the ravine. There were only three houses on the short street which was almost more like a lane. At the end of it was the Current River Ravine. An uneven slope, relatively steep at the top and gentler at the bottom, led to the riverbed. On the opposite side a gentler pitch led up to an empty lot where, in the winter, kids would bring their toboggans and sleds to go sliding. The adventurous ones would climb up the Peter Street side and get a really exciting ride down to the frozen riverbed. In the spring, when the snow melted, Current River was high and dangerous, but as spring gradually gave way to summer, it would shrink to not much more than a wide, shallow trickle which could easily be crossed by stepping from stone to stone. For good parts of the year, the ravine was a great shortcut.

It was also the site of the incident.

The incident was something Gino didn't like to think about. It had happened in June, on a hot, overcast Saturday afternoon. He had delivered the papers early, but hadn't started his collection immediately after. His mother had needed him at home, to look after Maria for the morning. When his mom returned home in the middle of the afternoon, he had grabbed his collection cards and his pouch with two dollars of loose change and he had set off.

A few customers hadn't been home and Mrs. Besson had kept him for five minutes to complain that he was supposed to collect in the morning, but overall it had gone well. He had finished the houses on Peter Street and turned onto the small dead-end street to take the short cut across the ravine. For some reason, once in the lane, he had taken the money pouch from his pocket, loosened the drawstring, and thrust his right hand into the coins as if he could start separating the nickels from the quarters and dimes.

Suddenly, on the middle of the street, he found himself confronted by Duke Shewchuck. Duke was two years older than Gino and stood at least a head higher although at school they were in the same class. At school, Gino, like most other kids, avoided Duke as much as possible. Duke was big, stupid, and mean.

"Sounds like you got a lot of money in that bag."

"It's not mine. It's the newspaper collection."

"You deliver newspapers?"

"Yeah."

"Must make money doing that?"

"A bit."

"What are you doing here?"

"I'm just cutting across the ravine."

"This isn't your street. It's gonna cost you to cut across."

Gino didn't know what to say. He was uncomfortable with Duke's looming bulk just inches from him. He wished he'd kept his pouch in his pocket. He wished he'd been looking up instead of playing with his money.

"It's gonna cost you fifty cents to cut across."

"This isn't my money. It belongs to the newspaper. I won't cut across. I'll go around."

Gino took a step back but he wasn't quick enough. Duke's big hand grabbed Gino's shirt.

"It's gonna cost you to go back too."

"It's not my money. I'm not giving you any of it."

Gino tried to pull away, but Duke's other hand flashed out—a big, heavy fist and Gino was on the ground. Instinctively, he clutched the money pouch close to his body and rolled to get away but Duke's knees came down hard on Gino's chest and stomach. He felt the wind go out of him and he gasped for breath.

Then, as suddenly as it had started, it was over and Gino was alone on the dusty gravel. Duke was gone and so was his money pouch. Gino pulled himself to his knees and through tear-filled eyes reached out for the few dozen coins that lay scattered in the dust. His ribs hurt and so did his stomach. He didn't dare touch his face, but he could tell that he had a swollen lip. He felt pain and loss that went far beyond the bruises on his body and the missing money.

The same evening, when she got back from work, Graziella had walked him right back to the small lane. She had knocked loudly on Duke Shewchuck's back door. The man who eventually came to the door was big and fat. He carried an open beer bottle in his left hand and looked even meaner than Duke.

"I don't know nothing about it," he told them. "Duke's not here." Gino could tell that Graziella didn't believe him but she was suddenly as powerless as he had been. On the way home Gino explained again that he hadn't lost all the money. He had eight dollars in bills tucked into his left sock. Graziella looked at him and then they both laughed.

❧

Gino never took the short cut any more when he was collecting. If he hesitated just a moment this morning it was because he wondered how quick the short cut would be. If lots of kids had gone sliding yesterday there would be a good path going up the other side. Otherwise it would be a very hard trudge up the hill and it would be easier to go back to Algoma Street.

The lane hadn't been ploughed since Monday's storm. Still, at least a few cars had ventured through because ruts ran down the middle of the street. Gino noted that a car had already used the lane that morning because there were fresh, new tracks in the ruts. There was a little more light now. Gino decided that he would go to the end of the lane. He might be able to see if there were signs that kids had been sliding. If so, he would put his remaining few papers into one bag and use the other as a toboggan. He knew from experience that it wasn't as good as a piece of cardboard, but it would do. If no one had been sliding yesterday, he would retrace his steps and go around by Algoma.

Gino had no deliveries to make and he tucked his mitten-bound hands as best he could into his coat pockets. He walked down one of the ruts and, because it was second nature to do so, he noted who had cleaned their walkways and who hadn't. The first house had cleaned the walkway, but not their driveway. The second house had cleaned only the driveway. The last house, the only one with a light on, was Duke's place. The house was small and even in the winter looked shabby and neglected. The walk leading to the front door hadn't been cleaned all winter. But the ruts in the road led to the Shewchuck's double driveway and part of it had been cleaned. There were always two or three old cars or beat up pick-up trucks in the Shewchuck's drive-way and the vehicles seemed to change all the time. This morning, two large mounds in the driveway were proof that at least two of the cars hadn't moved since the storm. The part of the driveway closer to the house had just been cleaned. Gino could tell because even the new snow was gone. The car that had left tracks in the lane had come from the Shewchuck driveway. It seemed to Gino that whoever had cleaned the snow had quit in the middle of the job. The snowblower stood silent, half way down the driveway, its open jaw waiting to devour its next meal.

Gino turned his attention back to his path. The wheel ruts went no further but, under the fresh snow, footsteps had already beaten an uneven path towards the end of the street. Gino knew what that meant. Kids had gone sliding yesterday. Perhaps, if he was lucky, he might even find a good piece of cardboard. The sky was getting lighter by the minute and he'd probably be able to see fairly well as he slid down the ravine. That was when Gino found the thumb.

It was odd how he found it. What he first saw was a hole in the fresh snow. The hole, a dark shadow really, was half a step from the pathway. It looked a little like a hole that would be left by the butt end of a hockey stick. But, Gino thought, who would bring a hockey stick to go sliding? If it were a hockey stick, wouldn't he have seen a lot of holes? His curiosity had been piqued and, instead of walking by it, he looked more closely. He brushed away the new snow around the small hole, and stared dumbstruck when he realized what it was he was looking at.

It took him a full moment to bend down and pick up the thumb.

He looked at it as it lay inert in the palm of his mittened hand. It was, unmistakably, a man's thumb. It was big. It had been cleanly sliced just above the first knuckle and had a stumpy look to it, but even so it seemed to Gino that it was twice the size of his own thumb. There was black under the nail and the creases in the skin were also black as if it hadn't been washed in a long time. There was no hint of blood at the severed end. As he looked at it, Gino thought of his science text book and drawings in it that looked just like this. All that was missing was the labeling: bone, blood vessel, nerve, skin.

Gino stood with the severed digit long enough that he was suddenly conscious of the cold. It was a nice morning as long as you kept moving. If you stopped, you'd freeze.

Yet, Gino didn't move. His body was paralyzed by the barrage of questions in his brain. What should he do with it? Whose was it? How did it get here? He knew, because he often read the paper he delivered daily, that doctors were now able to sew on people's arms and legs. Just last week, there'd been the story of a Doctor MacLeod in Detroit who had reattached a man's severed hand. But if somebody lost a thumb, wouldn't that person look for it?

The same way that the sky suddenly goes from dark to light, the questions in Gino's head suddenly all had answers, even though one of the answers he really didn't like at all.

There was definite light in the sky when he knocked on the Shewchuck's back door. He knocked with his bare knuckles and he knocked loudly three times. A part of him was relieved when he turned away from the closed door. He hadn't prepared any words at all. He could have said something silly: "Hi, I was wondering if you'd lost one of your thumbs." He was glad he didn't have to see any of the Shewchucks. It actually made it easier to do what he knew he had to do. The first thing, as he moved quickly down the path towards the ravine, was to scoop up a few handfuls of fresh snow and make a hard ice ball with the severed thumb in the middle.

My Cousin Bruce

We come back from the funeral 'cause of what happened to
Théo's pants and we're there sitting in the car and waiting
for Théo. And I can tell Maman's upset because they were
his only good pants and Son Père is upset too 'cause he and
Maman are both looking straight ahead and not talking to
each other. I don't know for sure but I think Son Père is
upset because by the time we get back to the church basement for the wake it'll almost be time for us to come back
home and do chores and Son Père won't have much time to
go out behind the church and drink Mon Oncle Reynald's
whiskey blanc.

It's hot in the car, even with the windows open like they
are and I think maybe everyone's in a bad mood. Lucie, I
think, is mad because Angélique is sitting in the front with
Maman and Son Père. When we leave the church yard she
wants to be in the front so Roméo Blanchette can see her.
But she doesn't come to the car right away. She stands around
on the church steps waiting for
Roméo to look at her and Angélique
is quick to get to the car and she
takes the seat in the front before
Lucie. So Lucie has to sit in the
back with Théo and Geneviève and

me and Geneviève has put on so much perfume that she would scare away even the skunks, and Théo is so big that we are all squished together and by now we probably all smell like Geneviève, although I was lucky to get the other window seat and at least I have some fresh air to breathe.

So we sit in the car and wait and no one can understand why Théo is taking so long to change his pants. I know I cannot laugh because Maman or Son Père will reach back and slap me and so I try not to think about Théo and the way, as he goes through the church door, with the casket on his shoulder, and him at the back with Mon Oncle Albert, and because Théo is big all around, he goes too close to the door. Somehow the pocket of his pants catches on the door latch. I am with Maman right behind him and when his pants pocket catches he knows it but he cannot stop because all the others are walking with the coffin and he has to keep up, or the coffin with Grand-maman will fall. The pants, which are his only good pair of pants, are too tight on him because they were bought for Grand-père's funeral last year, and Théo has grown since then. They rip. And we are all so quiet going out of the church with Grand-maman's coffin that I think everyone must hear the pants rip and there is Théo's black pants with a long strip of white underwear and pink skin halfway down his leg, and Théo needs two hands to hold the coffin but he wants to take one hand to hold the strip to hide his underwear. And Maman lets go of my hand and rushes forward and tries to hold the strip up. Now Théo walks like a duck from side to side and Maman is like the windshield wipers on the car. But this is Grand-maman's funeral and everyone must stay serious and pretend that we don't see Théo's underwear.

And when the coffin is put into the hearse, Théo's face is all red and he stands sideways so his underwear will not show.

When the back door of the hearse is closed and it pulls away and we all go to the car to follow it to the cemetery, Théo walks sideways like a red crab. He is the pallbearer but Guillaume, who is Mon Oncle Reynald's second oldest son and also my cousin, is the one who brings the coffin out of the hearse when we get to the cemetery and Théo stands back by the car and not with everybody else who throws a handful of dirt on the coffin to bury Grand-maman.

But I try not to think of any of those things because I know they will only make me laugh and I do not want Maman to reach back and slap me.

I am trying to keep my mind blank and only wondering why Théo is taking so much time to get changed when there is a car that comes into the yard. I wonder who it could be, because it is big and new and very expensive and I do not know anyone in Sainte-Éloge-de-Cushing who could possibly own a car like this. We all look and when the car door opens and the driver steps out, Son Père bellows, "*Ben, maudit!*" which is something he is not supposed to say, especially today when Grand-maman has just been buried. He jumps out of our car and runs over and takes the man by the shoulders and gives him a big hug and I know that this must be an old friend. Then Maman gets out and she too goes to see him.

Now the other door opens and a blond woman gets out and she is thin like a calf and when Théo finally comes out of the house, he too goes to see these new people and when he stands beside the blond woman, she looks even more thin, like a calf that is sick.

"*Ah ben coudonc!* It's Mon Oncle Robert!" says Lucie and she pushes me out of the car and runs over to where they are all standing. Only Angélique stays in the car because she does not want to lose the front seat.

The older ones know Mon Oncle Robert, but for me he is a stranger although I have heard of him because long ago he crossed over the lines and has become very rich and now he is back because Grand-maman has died. And he has come with his family which is his wife and a son who is also very thin and very tall but I am told his name is Bruce and he too is ten years old.

It is because of this that when we finally leave the yard to go back to the church basement for Grand-maman's wake, that I am invited to ride in the shiny black car which is a Chrysler Imperial and I know it is a rich man's car. I sit in the back with my cousin. The seat is soft and I sink so deep into it that I wonder if I will ever come out. Inside the car, the windows are closed but the air is fresh and cool like spring time. And there is space. In this car, I could say anything and no one could reach back to slap me.

Mon Oncle Robert is the way Théo would be if Théo talked a lot. He asks me so many questions my head becomes dizzy. But his wife is quiet until she says to her husband, "Doesn't anybody here speak English?" and I can tell she is not happy with her husband so, because I am raised to be polite, I say to her, "Of course, Madame, I speak English. How do you do?" I don't understand why, but Mon Oncle Robert laughs and my cousin Bruce, who is as quiet as his mother, looks at me and smiles in a funny way, but, because he is from the other side of the lines, I think to myself, that is the way the people from there must smile.

We are at the church long before Son Père because the Chrysler Imperial makes no noise but goes faster than any car I have ever seen. At the church basement, there are all of my Mon Oncles and Ma Tantes and all my cousins, and of course almost all of the village as well because my Grand-maman was the oldest woman in Sainte-Éloge-de-Cushing and it is not every day that there is a funeral for someone important like that.

I can see that Mon Oncle Robert's wife is very anxious and nervous about all these people around her and she holds Bruce by the shoulder like she is afraid to lose him but Mon Oncle Robert tells her, in English, which is a language I understand very well because since I was eight I have been helping our neighbour, Mr. Wilbur Wright on his farm, although today, because of my Grand-maman's funeral his wife, who is very kind, told me not to come to help, he tells her not to worry.

"My little nephew," he says to me, in English so that his wife can understand, "will you stay with Bruce and keep an eye on him?"

"Of course," I say, "he is my cousin. We are family."

My cousin Bruce is not a big talker and so far he has said only "Hello" to me. He has not said, how do you do, even though that is the polite thing to say but maybe it is not that way on the other side of the lines, so I accept that he has just said hello.

There is a big crowd in the church basement. It seems to me that the entire village of Sainte-Éloge is there, even some of the English, even though they are Protestant. I wonder if they will be excommunicated for being here in the Catholic church, although this is only the basement so maybe they are safe.

I ask my cousin Bruce if he wants that we go and get some food and drink because if we wait too long perhaps there will be nothing left. He shrugs his shoulders which are all made of bone and looks at me with the eyes of a sad dog.

"Come," I tell him, "be happy. After all, this is a wake. It is no time to be sad."

As usual, he says nothing. But he follows me to the banquet table where all the food is set out. The line is already long, but Ma Tante Madeleine is half turned around talking to Mme Michaud who is behind her and she is so busy talking she does not see us and we slip in front of her and we fill our plates. Or at least I do. Bruce keeps asking me, what is this and what is that? He takes very little of the food and I understand why he is so thin like his mother.

We sit at a table where Laurier Renaud is sitting with Eugénie Larochelle, who, now that Grand-maman has gone to heaven, is the oldest person in all of Sainte-Éloge. I am very polite and ask if we may join them and I ask after their health but Eugénie Larochelle, it is well known, is deaf. Bruce eats very slowly so that I have a chance to go twice to get dessert before he has finished the few things on his plate.

After we have finished eating, and I am feeling quite full, I bring my cousin Bruce around the church basement to meet his cousins but Bruce only ever says hello. He never asks how do you do, and maybe the cousins do not know that this is the way it is on the other side of the lines and no one seems much interested in Bruce so that pretty soon I find the church basement is very noisy and crowded and I wonder if it might not be nicer outside. I think this too because I know Son Père and Théo will have to go home to do the chores and perhaps they will look for me to help because it will go faster if there are three and they will be able to come back sooner. It is not that I do not wish to help, but I have told Mon Oncle Robert that I will stay with my cousin Bruce and look after him and in his nice clothes he would not go well in our barn.

I do not want Mon Oncle Robert to worry, and especially not his wife, so I go halfway up the stairs and look until I can find Mon Oncle Robert and we go to him and tell him we will go outside for a short while. This is fine with him but his wife warns Bruce not to go far and to watch for cars and to not get dirty and so many other things that my head is almost dizzy and I wonder how Bruce can remember so much.

It is later than I thought and nowhere in the church yard do I see our car, which means Théo and Son Père have left to do chores. I see that Mon Oncle Reynald has the trunk of his car open and there are four or five men standing around, but after a minute they slowly start to make their way back to the church basement. Mon Oncle Reynald is the last of them and it seems to me that the trunk of his car is not all closed so after he has safely gone down to the church basement, I tell my cousin Bruce that he is in for a treat.

The car is parked in the back corner, next to the fields that belong to Napoléon Crèvecoeur. It takes us only a minute to cross the parking lot and I am curious to see if Mon Oncle's trunk really is open. My eyes were not mistaken, the trunk is not completely closed and when I open it a little more I see a blanket but there are bumps under the blanket and I ask my cousin Bruce if he has ever tasted *whiskey blanc*. Bruce does not know what *whiskey blanc* is and since I am polite and since I do not think that Mon Oncle Reynald will notice too much, I lift the blanket and see that there are at least five bottles staying warm under it. Some are full but there is one which has only a little bit of liquid left and I think that it will be enough to give Bruce a taste, and me too.

If we were men we would stand by the car and pass the bottle back and forth, but I think it is safer if we find another place. Already we have seen one or two people leave for they are acquaintances and not true friends of Grand-maman, so it is better for me and Bruce to go elsewhere. The school playground is on the other side of the church but it is not a good idea to go there because there are children there and even some cousins. I think it is better to go through Napoléon's field to his maple bush which is not very far.

This means we have to go through the barbed wire fence and even though I tell Bruce that I will hold up the top wire and he is to push down the middle wire and even though I show him how to climb through he is clumsy and catches his back on one barb and before he is through he catches his pant leg on another barb and I can see that his mother will not be pleased because the sharp metal has torn his nice clothing. But I say to myself, the damage is done and cannot be undone so I convince Bruce that there would be nothing gained by turning back now.

To my surprise, Napoléon Crèvecoeur has planted his field in oats and I know he would not want anyone tramping through his oats. But I have just convinced Bruce that there would be nothing gained by turning back so I tell myself that we are small and we will make such a small trail that no one will even notice. I tell Bruce to stay close behind me and to try to step in my footsteps. The oats are high and green and I can tell they will soon be ready to harvest. I am surprised at how big the field is and how far Napoléon's sugar bush seems to be. When I stop for a minute and look behind me, the church and the village seem very far away and the sugar bush is no closer.

It is too far to see who it is, but there are people coming out of the church basement. I squat down and tell Bruce to do likewise. Bruce asks what's wrong and because I don't want to worry him, I tell him it is time to take a sip of *whiskey blanc.* We are far away and the oatfield floats above our heads. I am about to unscrew the cap when Bruce lets out a scream that startles me and I fall backwards. I see that Bruce too has fallen and I can see that we have knocked down a good number of Napoléon's oat stalks. What has happened is that Bruce has seen a garden snake.

The damage to Napoléon's oats has been done and I hope that maybe there will be a big rain storm with lots of wind and what we have done will appear to be the work of wind and rain. I unscrew the bottle and pass it to Bruce and tell him to drink first. He looks at the bottle in his hand and I encourage him. With his sleeve he wipes the rim of the bottle but I think that maybe he should not have done that because I can see that the elbow of his jacket is quite dirty and I think maybe the whole arm of his jacket is that way because of the way he fell backwards into the oats.

I do not know how much my cousin Bruce drinks with his first swig because he coughs and chokes and I am afraid that he will drop the bottle and spill what is left. I grab it from his hand before something happens to it and I watch as he loses his balance and falls on yet more of Napoléon Crèvecoeur's oats. When he finally stops coughing and choking, I can see that his eyes are red with tears. He has made a lot of noise and I raise my head just above the sea of oats and look towards the church. There are men standing around Mon Oncle Reynald's car but they are just standing and not looking towards us. I watch them for a minute and I realize that we are quite safe as long as we stay down.

"Watch how I drink," I tell my cousin Bruce. I lift the bottle to my lips and take a small sip which tastes cool on my tongue before sliding like a flame down my throat. I have taken only a small sip and even though my throat is in flames I do not choke or cough.

"Try taking just a small sip," I tell my cousin.

"I don't like it," he says to me.

My cousin, I am sad to admit, is not only clumsy, but he is also very slow. "That doesn't matter," I explain to him. "Just take a small sip."

It takes a few minutes but eventually he does and even though he makes the face of a lemon in great pain, he does not choke this time and he hardly coughs at all.

"It tastes awful," he says.

"Of course," I tell him. "This is *whiskey blanc*, and it is made by our Oncle Reynald. It is the best in the entire village."

When I peek again over the oats I see that the men who were standing around Mon Oncle's car have gone back inside. We still have a few sips left in the bottle but I am no longer sure of going all the way to the sugar bush which is far off.

There is another place we could more easily reach. It is no more than four or five furlongs from where we stand if we veer off to the east. It is an old barn that Napoléon has not used since before I was born. It is clearly a much better place than the sugar bush for us to sit quietly and finish our drink.

We arrive and just in time because when I look back towards the church I again see people among the cars. Bruce and I sit down in the tall grass and lean back against the weathered barn. There is not much left in our bottle and even though he complains, my cousin Bruce drinks his share.

"Should we leave the bottle here or bring it back?" I ask my cousin.

He looks at me and after a long while he replies, "I don't know."

It is very nice where we are. The sky is still bright even though it is evening. There are swallows and I point them out to my cousin who does not know that swallows are birds.

I start to explain that there are many different types of birds and he stops me and says, "What was that?"

I listen and my cousin is right. We are not alone here. I push the bottle into the grass at the edge of the barn where it grows tallest and I prepare myself to run.

"No. Listen," says my cousin.

It is very strange and I cannot explain what I hear. I try to think what could be inside the barn, for that is where the noises are coming from. I think I hear someone cry, the way you cry when you are being hurt but then it is another sound, like a pig rooting in mud, and then we can almost hear what sounds like laughter and voices but I cannot make out the words. I am ready to leave but there is another cry and it is louder this time.

"We have to go help," says Bruce.

I look at him and it seems to me he is no longer skinny and clumsy. In the sunlight he looks tall and strong and brave. But maybe I am wrong because my head feels just a little dizzy.

"Come!" he orders me and we start going around the barn to look for the door. The sounds from inside come and go and come and go, sometimes louder, sometimes softer, and we walk around the three sides of the barn before we find the door because we have guessed wrong.

When we reach the door, we find that it has been rolled partially open, open enough that, if we wanted to, we could walk in. It is dark inside, even though we see patches of light because there are holes in the roof, and missing planks in the walls. Bruce hesitates for a moment but then we hear another sharp cry. Bruce reaches for the door but he is unable to push it open any further. The rollers on which the door is suspended are no doubt full of rust. I move beside him and, with the two of us pushing, the door begins to roll open with the loud, harsh, grating sound of rusted metal.

The door makes noise but there is another noise, a cry, but this one is different. It is a cry of surprise. Then a voice, a voice that is loud and angry, is calling out, *"C'est qui ça?"*

And a fraction of a moment later there is something in the half-shadows of the barn and it is big and it is moving towards us and Bruce and I turn and run.

We have not run far it seems to me when Bruce trips and falls. I look back and see that we are no longer being chased. I catch a glimpse of someone with a flapping shirt going into the darkness of the barn.

It is perhaps good that Bruce has fallen, even though he is now much more dirty than if he had done chores in our barn, because we have been running the wrong way, not towards the church, but away from it. The two of us squat in the oats to catch our breath and then, quite suddenly, Bruce spills all his supper onto Napoléon Crèvecoeur's oatfield. It is not too bad because he had only a small supper and there was only a little to spill onto his jacket. We have to stay put for several minutes because I can see that my cousin is now looking a strange colour between white and green. While we wait I peek over the oats to determine the best way to go around the barn and get back to the church, although as I think of it, I wonder if there is not someplace safer to go to clean Bruce up before I return him to his mother.

It is then that I see two people come out of the barn and I cannot be sure because they are moving quickly and are keeping themselves half hunched over but for a moment I wonder if it is not my sister Lucie that I have seen with Roméo Blanchette coming out of the barn.

When we get back to the edge of Napoléon's oatfield dusk is falling. I am thinking of what I will say to Mon Oncle Robert and his thin wife because my cousin Bruce does not look at all as he looked a few hours ago.

We have just climbed through the barbed wire fence when Bruce's mother appears in front of us. She looks at Bruce and puts her hand to her mouth and screams. She seizes him and pulls him into her arms with tears rolling down her face. Then Mon Oncle Robert is beside her, but before I can say a word, or before he can say a word, she yells at him.

"We're leaving! This minute!"

And I watch as they cross the church yard and climb into the big Chrysler Imperial and pull out of the yard. And until I am much older, that is the last time I see my cousin Bruce who lives across the lines.

The Shortened Version

Darren had discovered his hidey-hole the same afternoon his mom had dropped him off. He had noticed something that, in all the times he had been at his grandparents', he had never spotted before: a small door. There was a small door in the white-painted trellis that acted like a skirt to hide the empty space under the front veranda. The door looked just like the rest of the trellis and Darren would never have noticed it if it hadn't been slightly ajar. It was on the far side of the house and half-hidden by the neatly trimmed cedar hedge.

He had pulled gently and it had grudgingly opened a little wider. He had bent his head and looked down the dark crawlspace which, like the veranda, ran the whole length of the front of the house. Little lozenges of sunlight speckled the part of the sandy, dirt floor closest to the trellis. Darren stayed crouched and took a small, tentative step into this newly discovered dark space. The air felt different in here. It smelled old and dusty. As his eyes adjusted to the dark, the first thing he was conscious of were the cobwebs. Dust-thickened, they seemed to droop gently from the underside of the veranda floor like miniature clouds.

Darren waddled a few steps forward, tentatively swinging his left hand just in front of his head to brush away the offensive webs. He half recoiled from their soft touch and felt himself off balance. From his squatting position he put his right knee to the ground and he was surprised how cool the soil felt on his bare skin. He stayed genuflecting for a minute and realized there was no point brushing the cobwebs away for those that drooped from the planks above his head were matched by others that hung along the cement foundation of the house and on the inside of the trellis.

Darren was about to waddle forward when the scurrying sound of some unknown thing startled him. He stopped and sensed rather than saw something that seemed large and dark; although, in the diamond-strewn darkness he almost thought he saw a flash of white.

He hadn't gone any further under the veranda that day. Nor on any of the other times he had quietly slipped through the trellis door since then. After the second time his Grandma had scolded him and asked him where he'd been, his shorts and T-shirt were so full of dust and cobwebs. He hadn't told her, not out of deceit or dishonesty, but because she was carried away in her scolding and gave him no time to answer. It was after that incident that Darren had taken the whisk and spent the better part of half an hour cleaning a small space for himself in the corner closest to the door. Since then he'd furnished his secret space with a cardboard box in which he kept two old issues of *Owl Magazine* which had been left in the house long ago. He also had a book, *Muffet's Adventure,* which he'd brought from home and of which he'd only read only a page or two which he had opened at random. Recently, he had started to bring food here, cookies from the pantry that he put aside in a plastic container, the way a trapper in the far north might lay in a cache of dried caribou meat.

The corner under the veranda was where Darren had retreated when the dog arrived. The dog, which belonged to his Aunt Tiffany, was a Jack Russell terrier. That was the first thing she had told him when she came by to drop the dog off.

"He's a Jack Russell terrier," she had said. "A purebred Jack Russell terrier and he's worth a lot of money. He's not used to being here so if it's you who takes him for a walk, you keep him on the leash at all times. Even if you go to the park, don't let him off the leash to run around. He doesn't know you and he might not come back to you. And keep him away from other dogs. He's not that big and I don't want him getting hurt. But, um…but it would be better if you didn't walk him at all."

She had put emphasis on the word "you," and Darren had backed away a half step from his aunt. He didn't know why she thought him incapable of walking her dog but all of a sudden, he felt that he really didn't want to walk the dog, even if it was a purebred Jack Russell terrier.

Standing in the front hall, Darren looked up at his Aunt Tiffany. He knew she had been a teacher and now she was the principal of her school. Darren felt really glad that she wasn't the principal of his school. He looked away from his aunt and down at the dog and saw that the dog's dark eyes were looking up at him belligerently, as if to ask, "What are you doing here?"

His Grandma had come down the stairs at that point and Darren had taken the opportunity to quietly slip away. He hadn't said goodbye to his Aunt Tiffany even though he knew she was leaving on a trip somewhere. He had gone through the kitchen and out the back door and then around the house and into his special space under the veranda.

That had been over a week ago. That first day it was his Grandpa who had walked the dog but when he came back from his evening walk he announced, "I'm not going to walk out there like an old fool with that yappy midget of a dog. And you won't believe what happened when I got home!"

His Grandma had walked the Jack Russell the next few days. The task had fallen to Darren one morning when she had an appointment. "Just go around the block," she had told him, "and take this plastic bag so you can pick up after him. Like this," and she had shown him how a plastic bag can become a glove and then a small, well wrapped package to be dropped in the garbage.

It wasn't hard walking the Jack Russell, even if the dog did tend to give a strong tug on his leash every few steps as he tried to run off after a bird or a squirrel or, much more often, some phantom prey. Darren remembered his aunt's words and he couldn't understand what was so special about the dog. Darren didn't find the animal especially attractive. As his Grandpa had said, it didn't look like much more than an overgrown rat. Nor did the dog show anything which could be mistaken for endearing behaviour. He had a tendency to nip at your ankles when he wanted something; not that it was easy to know what he wanted. He'd nip at your ankle, scoot back two paces and then stand looking at you and you had to guess if it was feeding time, or if he needed water or if he wanted to go out.

Another thing: he would suddenly start barking fiercely for no apparent reason and he had a surprisingly loud bark for a small dog. The day he arrived, at supper time, he had made everybody jump by suddenly launching into a fit of strident barking. Grandpa had dropped his fork and Grandma had knocked over her glass of water, which, thankfully, was almost empty.

Darren didn't think the dog was very bright either. Once, for example, the dog had wrenched his arm as he lunged unexpectedly off to the right and started barking furiously. Darren didn't know what had set the dog off until he glanced at the picture window of the house in front of which they were passing. A cat sat placidly in the window, staring with bored disinterest as Darren tugged at the leash of the demented Jack Russell.

Still, Darren was careful. He always had the leash wrapped around his wrist so even if it slipped out of his hand, the leash would still be attached to his arm. The few times he noticed larger dogs, he pulled the Jack Russell along quickly to avoid any canine confrontation. The trick was to keep a short leash. For some reason, Aunt Tiffany had bought a bright red leather leash that was a good fifteen feet long.

When they got back home, as when they left the house, Darren liked to keep an especially short leash. Twice already, the dog had managed to start digging in one of the flower beds. The first time, it had happened to Grandpa, and was probably part of the reason he had refused to walk the dog anymore. Back from his walk, grandpa had noticed a fallen branch and instead of putting the dog in the house, he had slipped the leash on a fence picket. A moment later he had seen clumps of dirt flying over the lawn as the Jack Russell burrowed into the rich dark soil without heed for the begonias and snapdragons which had been doing so well.

The other place the Jack Russell seemed to want to dig was under the veranda, on the driveway side of the house, the side opposite the small door. One morning, as he set out on his walk with the dog, his grandma had called to him to wait. She had something for him to drop off at Mrs. Tremblay's. Darren was waiting patiently, standing in the driveway and staring at the clouds, when he felt a tug on the leash. He spun around to find that the Jack Russell was behind the trimmed cedar bush that stood like a sentinel near the veranda. With his nose as much as his paws he was starting to burrow under the trellis. Ever since then, if he had enough leash, the Jack Russell would make a beeline for that spot.

As it turned out, that was the spot where the dog was sprayed. Or at least, the spot where Darren was pretty sure the dog was sprayed. Everybody was always careful about opening and closing doors so the Jack Russell wouldn't run outside (although Grandpa said if the dog got run over, it would sure save a lot of trouble). The dog probably would never have gotten outside, and gotten sprayed, if Grandpa hadn't tried to fix the outside faucet that fed the garden hose. The faucet, somehow, had snapped off in Grandma's hand. Grandpa had grumbled a little, but Darren could tell that he was secretly pleased to have a job to do. Unfortunately, what started as a broken faucet, a few hours later, grew into a pretty serious leak in the basement.

It was the plumber, going in and out through the side door, who inadvertently let the dog out.

Darren knew, almost right away, that the dog had escaped.

He had watched as his Grandpa had worked on the faucet. It was fun to watch almost any job that Grandpa had to do and often he, Darren, would be asked to hold something, or go down to the workbench to find some tool. Of course, once the water started leaking in the basement, Grandpa wasn't in a very good mood. When the plumber arrived Darren thought he could stay and watch but at a certain point Grandpa told him to run along and play. Sometimes with Grandpa you could just stand a little ways off and then he'd call you to go and get something for him, but this didn't feel like one of those times and Darren ended up wandering around to the other side of the house and opening the trellis door to his little hideaway. He picked up *Muffet's Adventure* but he hardly opened it before he put it back in the cardboard box.

He was sitting on the cool sand with his back against the equally cool cement foundation of the house, thinking about his Grandpa who was really nice some of the time but was just the opposite when he got upset. Darren could never tell what would upset his Grandpa. Darren tried to think back to times before this summer. For example, when they would come at Christmas, was Grandpa ever angry then? Darren couldn't be sure. He couldn't quite remember. Images came to his mind but Grandpa didn't seem to be in any of those images.

And when he, Darren, had arrived four weeks ago, how had Grandpa been? Darren wasn't perfectly sure, but he didn't think that Grandpa had been angry then. No, he hadn't. The first day, right after his mom had left, it had been Grandpa who had brought him to the Canadian Tire store and then they'd gone to the take-out and Grandpa had let him choose pizza for supper that night. It was Grandma who had seemed upset the first few days he was there, not an angry kind of upset but sad. Once he had looked up and seen her looking at him and all of a sudden a strange look had come over her face, and she had turned and rushed out of the room.

It was then, sitting in his hidey-hole, idly wondering if his mom was more like Grandma or more like Grandpa that Darren heard the Jack Russell barking. He sat up and the next thing he knew, through the crosshatch of trellis at the far end of the veranda, he could make out the form of the dog digging furiously. In a flash Darren scooted out the trellis door and ran around to the other side of the house to catch the dog and get him back inside.

By the time Darren ran around the hedge and half way across the front lawn, he realized that inside the house might no longer be the right place for the dog. The smell of skunk hit him several strides before he made it to the driveway. If it hadn't been for the smell, the sight of the dog on the driveway might have been almost funny. The Jack Russell was alternately barking and whimpering, rushing forward a few steps and then retreating while trying with his paws to scrape the invisible, offensive smell from his nostrils and snout.

The plumber, followed by Grandpa, came out the side door and promptly took several steps back towards the garage and back yard, as if staying away from the dog might protect them from the scent of skunk. Darren heard the dining room window slam shut and saw his Grandma's angry face turning away.

"There's just a bit left for me to do," the plumber said to Grandpa, "but nothing's leaking anymore so I think I'll come back and finish up on Monday. Smell should be gone by then. You don't mind if I leave a few tools down in the basement? I'll pick them up next time. I shouldn't need them over the weekend. I can go round the other side of the house, can't I?"

It took quite a while after the plumber had left for Grandpa to actually go and pick up the dog. He had quieted down but both his eyes and his nose were clearly bothering him. He smelled awful. Grandpa carried him at arm's length, not to the house, but to the small shed behind the garage. He shut the dog in the shed and, without the slightest tinge of anger in his voice called out to Darren, "Want to come and buy tomato juice with me?"

Surprisingly, the next day, when Darren thought of the trellis door that, in his rush to get the Jack Russell, he had left open, there was no hint of skunk spray at all in the crawlspace under the veranda.

It was three or four days after the incident with the skunk that the Jack Russell was killed. It was the middle of a hot, sleepy afternoon. Darren had been ensconced in his hidey-hole and had only just come into the kitchen. He had gone to the pantry and was just reaching for the box of cookies when someone rang the bell at the kitchen door.

"Hello, young man," said the plumber. "Is your grandpa home?"

"Come in," said Darren. "I'll go get him."

Before Darren had taken two steps towards the swinging door that led from the kitchen to the hallway, his Grandpa arrived, saw who it was and stopped in his tracks.

"Ah, Benoît! Let me get my wallet."

But as his grandpa went out the door, the Jack Russell scooted in.

"Hey, there's the little skunkhound," said the plumber with a smile. "Did you get all the smell off?"

As Darren started to answer, the Jack Russell barked at the plumber and then rushed at him and nipped at his ankle.

"Hey," yelped the plumber lifting his leg out of the way. The dog backed off a few paces and stared at the plumber with malevolent eyes. Then, as Benoît tentatively put his left leg back on the floor, the Jack Russell sprang forward again and latched onto Benoît's pant leg, growling through clenched teeth. Benoît gave a cry of surprise and lifted his leg with the

Jack Russell firmly attached. He yelled at the dog to get off and shook his leg again and again, cursing the dog as he did so. The dog was small, but its weight was enough to cause the plumber to lose his balance and as he jerkily turned to catch himself on the counter, the Jack Russell, as if he'd been shot from a miniature cannon, arced across half the kitchen into the fridge door and slid lifeless to the floor.

In the moment of stunned silence that Darren and the plumber looked at each other, Grandpa walked in holding his open wallet in one hand and counting off bills with the index finger of the other. "Here," he said, taking out several bills, "I think this is right."

"I'm very sorry," said the plumber, making no effort to take the money.

"About what?" said Grandpa.

All three of them (Darren last) ended up touching the dead carcass to search for a heartbeat that wasn't there. It took a few minutes to describe what had happened. The plumber, pleading his innocence, and Darren, as the only eyewitness, recounted the last ninety seconds of the Jack Russell's life a couple of times over.

"So…I'm very sorry," said the plumber. "If I could make it up to you…buy you a new dog?"

"No!" said grandpa. "No, it wasn't your fault at all. Here, Benoît, here's what I owe you for your time and here…" he said putting two more bills in Benoît's hand.

"But," said Benoît. "Why?"

"Your pant leg looks torn," said Grandpa. "Take it. Get yourself another pair of overalls. I'll look after the dog. And, Benoît, we won't mention anything about this, ok?"

The plumber left and Grandpa turned to Darren and looked at him for a minute. "You know," said Grandpa. "You know what happened, don't you?"

"Yah, I guess," said Darren.

"You know that all these little hyperactive dogs have tricky hearts, don't you?"

"They do?" said Darren.

"And that's what happened to this poor little fella. His heart just up and gave out."

"It did?" said Darren.

"So, when your Aunt Tiffany comes back tomorrow, it might be best if we just tell her the shortened version of the story, that the dog just had a heart attack and dropped dead on the kitchen floor. What do you think?"

Darren looked at his Grandpa. He didn't know what to think, but he knew he trusted his grandpa. "Yah," he said, "I guess so."

"It'll be easier on everyone, I think," said Grandpa. "Sometimes, the less said, the better. Now, we'll have to bury the little fellow. What do you think of the flowerbed? Go call your Grandma to come down and ask her to bring an old towel or something that doesn't have to come back."

Failure All Over Him

"Damn!" he uttered, not to himself under his breath, but aloud.

"Sir! You're not supposed to say that."

Even as he heard the laughing words, little Rebecca Toussaint slipped through the door he was just pushing ajar, and sprinted around the corner, her laptop case swinging wildly at the end of her outstretched arm. A second later he heard a car door slam heavily shut and a patch of wet pavement was suddenly illuminated before a pick-up truck emerged from behind the school, splashed along the short drive and disappeared up the street.

Rebecca had surprised him. He had just said good night to Liz, who, as far as he could tell, was the only other teacher still in her classroom. He had also waved at Gaétan, at the

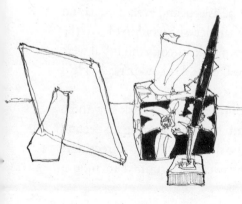

end of the hall, waiting patiently to lock up. Otherwise, he'd thought the school was empty. It was going on ten o'clock on a parents' night that had officially run from five to nine.

"Damn!" he said again, although this time, just in his head.

The rain was falling heavily, the drops exploding on the slick asphalt, sending droplets two or three centimetres back up into the air. He couldn't have said why, but he knew the rain was as cold as it was heavy. He would be soaked and shivering before he took twenty steps.

Not tonight, he pleaded, not tonight.

It had been an inconceivable, an unimaginable day. He felt bruised, as if he'd taken a physical beating. He felt as if he'd somehow been eviscerated and, if he dared to look down, he would see a dark hole where his stomach had been.

He hesitated. Perhaps the rain would ease off, diminish to a light drizzle. He wondered when it had started raining, and how it was that he could have been unaware of it. In the half-open door, he could feel how cold the outside air really was.

For a moment he wondered if he could phone home and ask Val to come and pick him up. It was such a short drive. It would take no more than a few minutes round trip. But the baby might or might not be asleep, and even if Val could easily plunk the baby in the carrier, she wouldn't leave the twins alone. Would it be fair to wake them? And if Val were asleep, he wouldn't want to wake her. He couldn't call. He'd have to do this on his own.

He looked at the rain falling out of the dark sky and a line from MacBeth came into his head. During his second or third year of teaching, he'd found himself directing a group of sixth-formers who were determined to mount

MacBeth. What came to him was a picture of a skinny, awkward boy—Teng—as Banquo, reciting his lines:

Tis strange
and oftentimes, to win us to our harm,
the instruments of darkness tell us truths,
win us with honest trifles, to betray's
. in deepest consequence.

He suddenly wondered if he had been won by trifles? Had everything—his immense good fortune, of which he was conscious, and for which he was grateful—been granted him just to bring him here, unable to move one way or the other?

ᘒ

They had arrived in the Townships only a few days after confirming Val's pregnancy. The Townships were a revelation to him—a little corner of the country he'd never heard of, nor even imagined existed. Ironically, the trip to Canada had already been planned; Val's parents were celebrating their fortieth wedding anniversary.

The pregnancy had put everything in a far different light. Neither of them could imagine bringing a child home into their small apartment. Neither could imagine raising a child in the mass of humanity that crushed up almost against their apartment door. The exotic East had been fine for them, first individually, and then as a couple, for almost a decade, but somewhere over the Pacific they agreed they were flying home to Canada, as Val put it, to nest.

Unlike the other trips they'd taken, aside from the weekend of the fortieth anniversary, they'd made no plans at all as to how to spend their six weeks in Canada. The job hunt had started less than twelve hours after they'd landed in Montreal. They were looking for a job for him. Val was going to be a stay-at-home mom, at least for the first seven or eight years. They thought his chances would be best in the Ottawa area, where, right after graduating from Carleton, he had taught for a year. Living in Ottawa, they'd be a short four hours from Val's parents. If they were lucky, they thought, they might even find a school for him a bit closer.

One afternoon, a day or two after the fortieth, they'd driven to Craigsville, to visit some cousins. Val's aunt, anxious to show off her exotic niece from the Far East, had invited a few neighbours over. The afternoon cup of coffee stretched into something of an impromptu, multi-generational, homecoming party that lasted till late at night. A week later, out of the blue, he got a phone call.

"They're looking for someone at one of the high schools," a voice told him. "I'm going to give you a number to call at the school board. Use my name as a reference."

Albert Lisgar was a friend of Val's aunt. He wasn't perfectly sure which of the people he'd met at the party was Al, but Albert Lisgar, among other things, was a school board commissioner.

The interview, a day after Al's phone call, had been almost perfunctory. Hardly two weeks after landing in Canada, they had found their job! And, unexpectedly, in the most emotionally perfect place that Val could imagine. At the end of August he'd start teaching English—he would have to learn to call it Language Arts—less than an hour's drive from Val's parents' place.

Just as improbable, as unexpected, was the manner in which they had found their home a few weeks later. They had driven to Sherbrooke with the day's editions of *La*

Tribune and *The Record*, and with a city map that still felt crisp and new. It was their second or third scouting expedition but they didn't feel in any rush. They were confident—especially Val—that they were going to find the perfect apartment in the perfect neighbourhood. They might even find a house to rent. With luck, Val said, maybe in Lennoxville. She had done her university at Bishop's and Lennoxville was something of a second home. That morning however, Val had toured him around the shaded streets of *le Vieux Nord* and they had stopped at Howard Park to stretch their legs for a few minutes. It was there the dominoes started to fall.

For, if they hadn't stopped at Howard Park, they wouldn't have met Barbara, who was one of Val's old room-mates. They wouldn't have gone to Barb's for lunch and so they wouldn't have met Kevin St. Pierre, the carpenter who was working on Barb's front veranda. Nor would they have met his sister, Solange, who needed a ride to Saint-François de Cushing, which was only a very slight detour on their way home to Val's parents' place. And if they hadn't struck up such a friendship with Solange on the way home, they wouldn't have stopped at her house, just for a minute. They wouldn't have met Solange's neighbour, Mrs. McGiven, who heard their story and said, "My, it's too bad you didn't get a job here because there'd be the perfect house for you just down the street. I was just talking to Jim Lefebvre. He wants to sell his place."

They weren't looking for a house to buy. They had never even talked, in any kind of serious way, about buying a house, so there was no explicitly logical reason for them to walk to the end of the block with Solange and Mrs. McGiven to look at a century-old, two-storey, clapboard house painted white and pink, sitting on an unexpectedly large lot. Jim

Lefebvre, as chance would have it, was standing outside his front door and was very glad to give them a tour of his house and yard. There were trees and hedges, and ample room for a serious vegetable garden. The back door opened onto an enclosure that had long before been a dog run and which, in all ways, was a perfect outdoor playpen for the child they were expecting. The house was full of light. The hardwood floors occasionally creaked. They walked from one room to another until they found themselves in an attic that seemed to have come out of a long-ago storybook.

They had left home that morning with the intention of looking at rental properties. They returned home almost certain that they were going to buy a house.

"*C'est une vieille maison,*" his father-in-law had said. Since then, he had come to understand what those laconic words actually meant. The windows were drafty and—for them—prohibitively expensive to replace. The walls were poorly insulated and kept a superannuated furnace running from early fall to late spring. The wiring was old; in the summer the radiator valves were sometimes leaky. Under multiple layers of fading wallpaper, the plaster was cracked and fragile.

"*C'est pas l'ouvrage qui manque,*" Marcel had warned, looking at the house with his experienced carpenter's eye, "*mais 'est ben faite.*" Meredith too, had given her guarded encouragement. By the time they made that second, formal visit, they were both in love with the house, in love with the promise it held, in love with the sudden, unexpected course their life had taken.

Not that many things went exactly as they'd envisioned them. The child they were expecting turned out to be twins and parenthood brought an extensive and varied set of new demands for which they were in no way prepared. The house seemed always to need something repaired or replaced, and it was depressingly expensive to heat. Their single salary never managed to stretch as far as they would have expected and sometimes needed. The hardest thing though, for him, had been the shock of his new school. The students he faced in his classes—compared to those he'd been teaching for the last decade—were like an alien species. It was as if he had somehow stepped half a century back in time. He didn't want to call them slow, or simple, because he recognized intelligence and sensitivity in them. But they weren't what he was used to. Often, his students gave him answers, or asked questions, which made him wonder if they'd ever had any formal education at all. His days of receiving occasional letters expressing thanks from former students who'd gone on to Cambridge or Princeton were over.

That first year, when he wasn't being woken by one of the twins, he was waking up from strange and disturbing dreams. In one he was on a race horse, an animal which moved as effortlessly and smoothly as a flying carpet. It was an important race and he was well ahead. Then, in the dream, he had to mount another horse. This second animal was a huge work horse, and even though he was kicking it with his heels and slapping its neck, the lumbering animal seemed content to amble along heedless of its rider. At the finish line, he found that the race was long over and everyone was gone. He was all alone.

At the end of that first year, he applied for a posting for a Grade 6 class at Abenaki Elementary. When he got the job, it was as much a cause for celebration as the job at the high school had been. Abenaki was less than a ten-minute walk from the pink and white house instead of an hour's drive. It represented savings in time and money, both of which were in short supply.

He'd always imagined that at some point he'd settle in one school and finish out his career. He'd just never expected it would be a small primary school in a rural backwater in an unknown corner of Quebec. Academically speaking, Abenaki represented a very modest, very humble calling. Strangely enough, much as this had bothered him that first year at the high school, at Abenaki it didn't bother him in the least. He quite welcomed it, as if he were a medieval monk devoting his life through humble labour to a greater cause.

The corollary was the surprising part, and that was how much he enjoyed small-town life and how happy he was with family life. He was aware that he had somehow acquired not just children, but a set of grandparents that went with them. He was conscious that for the first time since early adolescence, he was part of a family; not a small nuclear unit, but a vast network that seemed to spread endlessly beyond his reach through both time and space. Val's parents and siblings and cousins had all somehow also become his.

And now, staring at the downpour that faced him beyond the open door, he wondered what he was going to do. He couldn't put any of this into words. He couldn't imagine how he could ever explain it to Val but he saw that everything, inevitably, was going to collapse. He marvelled at how quickly it had happened, at how unsuspecting and unprepared he had been for what now faced him.

❧

She had called him over the intercom as he was about to dash home for a quick bite to eat and a short moment to see Val and the twins, and the baby if he was awake.

"I wanted to see you, just for a minute," she had said, when he knocked at her door. "Have a seat. I'll go get the files."

She had left him sitting in her office, a small room which was much changed since Fred had left at the end of June. Fred's old oak desk had been replaced by a new one made of some hard, plastic laminate, and of an L-shaped design to accommodate a screen and keyboard. Where Fred's desk was inevitably hidden beneath an avalanche of papers, this one had not a single sheet. On its imitation-wood surface there was an upscale pen holder in black and gold, a small box of tissues and a framed photograph of a dog.

At that moment, he had been unsuspecting. He wasn't even curious as to why Maureen wanted to see him. He had only been anxious to get home. It was a short ten-minute walk home and a short ten-minute walk back. That didn't leave much time to see Val and the kids and have a quick supper. Still, if he was very lucky, he might even have five minutes to sit with *The Record* before getting back to school, enough to refresh him for the evening ahead.

Maureen had barely laid a dozen manila folders on the corner of the desk when there was a rap on the door. When he heard Janet's voice, his heart sank. Janet was the Union rep. Whatever she'd come for would take forever, and the more trivial the matter, the longer Janet would make it take. He crossed his fingers that Maureen would send her away so that he could get home as soon as possible.

Yet, he guessed that wouldn't be likely. The previous spring, after Fred had announced his retirement, the staff room buzzed quietly for weeks with speculation on his replacement. When Maureen had been named as the new principal, her name had meant nothing to him. Janet however was full of stories predicting woe. We would be

Maureen's third school in three years. In that time, her people skills and administrative zeal had earned her a nickname: the Rottweiler. If you were called into her office, Janet had warned, as likely as not, you could expect to leave in tears. He had taken Janet's stories with a good grain of salt. It was ironic, he now thought, how, of all the teachers on the staff, it was Janet who had become chummiest with the new principal.

He looked at the folders on the desk and a faint suspicion grew that they were not a good omen. He half-heard the voices of the two women at the door and he willed Janet to go away. It was to no avail. After a minute, Maureen pulled the door closed behind her and left him alone to stare at the framed photo of a singularly unattractive dog. As his impatience gnawed at him, the dog in the picture seemed to grow increasingly ugly. When Maureen finally returned, he stole a glance at the clock above the door and his heart sank.

"I wanted to see you about some of your students," she said as she slid behind her desk. "This first reporting session is the best time to warn parents if their children are at risk, and I think there are several in your class. As I hope you know, in this country, we don't fail children in Grade 6. I know you've taught somewhere overseas, where they probably do that. In this country, only in an exceptional case will a child be held back. We want to focus on success. Now, as I was saying, a lot of your students are at risk. If a child's going to be going to the Learning Centre next year, or follow the Modified Program at the high school, I always think it's best to let parents know right from the beginning of the year."

The surprise must have shown on his face.

"You're not in the habit of doing this?" she asked. "I started doing this when I was still teaching, and I made sure my Grade 6 teachers did it in my other schools. It makes it much easier for everyone later on, believe me."

It was a foreign idea to him and one that raised all sorts of questions, but he nodded. He just wanted to get home.

"There's something else I want to mention to you first," she continued, her hands loosely clasped together on the desk in front of her.

She paused for a long second before continuing. "The other week, you went to a workshop …"

He had. It was over an hour's drive there and an hour's drive back. He—and how many others?—had listened to a couple of criminally dull speakers from the ministry and attended an afternoon workshop which, in the end, proved more confusing than anything else. He had come home angry and resentful. It had felt like a wasted day; he had returned from the workshop with nothing tangible and, of course, he'd done none of the many things that had to be done in his own classroom.

"I understand that you made a comment at one point?"

"A comment?"

"It wasn't you? Didn't you attend the Cycle Three workshop last Friday?"

"Yes." He was trying to get his bearings. He was distracted by the framed picture on her desk. He could hardly remember last Friday. What comment had he made? And to whom?

"What I want to tell you," she said, "is that your words were…regrettable. They were very hurtful to your fellow teachers, in particular to Jennifer and Ellen who teach Grade 5…"

"What?" he protested, "I've never said anything about anyone."

Maureen made a show of taking a breath, as if to say to a young child, "I know you're lying, but I'm going to be patient."

He suddenly knew what this was about. He knew what comment she was referring to.

"What I said was, the kids who came into my class this year were a lot weaker than they were last year. They have problems reading even…"

Maureen raised her hand to cut him off. "So you admit it. At least that. No, you've said more than enough already. Just listen. What's done is done. It's unfortunate but that's the way it is. I hope that next time you'll think before you speak. We all want to work together as a team and you can't go off like a loose cannon making irresponsible comments about your fellow teachers. No. No. There's no need for you to say any more. I think you've already said more than enough. We'll end that conversation. We have parents arriving soon and I want to review your 'at risk' students, so we know what to say to parents tonight."

He turned his eyes to the photo of the snarling mongrel. The most resonant words he'd heard were "coming soon" and he thought that maybe, just maybe, if he could keep it short, he still might have time to jog home, even if it meant taking the car back to school.

He didn't want to think about the rest of his principal's words. There was something very wrong about them. But there had been things wrong with the workshop itself, which was really a long session selling the ministry's educational reform. (He had tried reading the four-hundred page document outlining the reform which the ministry had prepared and which had been nicknamed the Brick. It had been a failed attempt. The document was the antithesis of what writing was supposed to be—longwinded and full of obfuscation instead of being clear and to the point.) The idea was that, after the ministerial mandarin's presentation, the teachers in Grade 6 would be ready to implement the Reform—as they were required to do by law. The Reform was being implemented gradually, year by year.

At one point, the mandarin had stopped to take yet another sip of water, and casually asked if there were questions.

That was the comment Maureen had referred to. He had raised his hand and said that he had concerns. He explained that the students he had this year—students introduced to the Reform last year—had come to him with unexpectedly poor writing skills, were much weaker in math, and had far less general knowledge than the kids he had had the year before. The mandarin had put down his water bottle and waited a very long time before finally saying—untruthfully as it turned out—that he'd address the point later on.

Maureen was ploughing ahead with something else. She had pulled the pile of folders in front of her so they acted almost as a barricade between the two of them. She was listing off names of pupils in his class, instructing him to advise the parents of one that their child would be placed in the Learning Center next year, or the parents of another that their child would be a candidate for the Modified Learning Program at the regional high school.

He nodded. He nodded and willed her to go faster. He would say nothing. He wanted to get out of her office and go home. Even if it meant his supper would be no more than an apple eaten in the car on the way back to school, he wanted to get home.

He nodded perfunctorily and watched the original pile shrink while a new pile grew to block the framed photo. He nodded again as she moved the penultimate folder to its new pile. He was ready to nod once more and leap out of his chair. He'd say, very politely, "Thank you. If you don't mind, I'm going to rush home now and get a bite to eat."

The next thing he heard was Martin Thompson.

"Martin Thompson!" The exclamation was out of his mouth before he realized he'd spoken.

"Oh?" she said, looking not at him but at the papers she was slowly turning in the fat file folder on her desk. "Do you think he could handle the Modified Learning Program? You don't think he would fit better at the Learning Centre?"

"Martin Thompson is one of the smartest kids in the class. He's..." he started.

"Looks like he's got behaviour problems as well," she cut him off, her nose still in the folder. "Let's see, how old is he? No, he's right with his cohort. Most of this is behaviour-related, but, no, no, he has always been placed and not promoted. Now, what did you say about being bright?"

"He is. He's a very bright boy."

"Well," she plunged back into the folder. "I'm surprised to hear you say that. As I look at this file—see here: placed, promoted, that was Grade 2, placed, placed, placed. He's only passed once in five years of schooling. Would you say that's the mark of a bright student?"

"No," he said, and almost right away he realized that the question had been rhetorical, but he continued on. "No, but he's much brighter than average. He's not working maybe, but he's a very smart kid. He's very good at math, and he's got the vocabulary of someone finishing high school."

"You haven't seen his file, have you? You should have taken the time to look at it. I believe it was at the first staff meeting in August that I reminded teachers to check the files of all their students, but particularly the code red and code orange students. What was that, six, seven weeks ago? Didn't you know this boy is coded orange?"

He stared at her. He'd seen some of the other eleven folders, kids with problems of one sort of another that marked
them as special needs children, but Martin Thompson? He
knew that Martin Thompson was an angry child, and it was
easy to imagine teachers labelling him as a discipline problem.
Yet, the boy was so obviously full of potential, so quick-
thinking that it was impossible to equate him with the folder
lying open on the desk. What mattered now, though, was
that she had scored a serious body blow and both of them
knew it. She let the silence sit much longer than necessary
and then swung at him again, a blow which he saw too late
and only partially deflected.

"You say he's not working? What do you mean by that?"

"It's hard to get work out of him. He doesn't hand in
his homework...that is, not the complete homework
assignment. He won't do all his work. At least not
always."

"You said he doesn't hand in his homework?"

"Not all of it. Not always," he lied. "He doesn't always
get it all done."

She was back with her nose in the folder. "Have you sent
me any incident reports about that? I see lots of incident
reports—far too many—but I don't see any from this year.
Did you fill in an incident report for the homework that
was not done?"

He shook his head to say no.

"You do know that a child that doesn't do his homework
is supposed to get an incident report? That is not only a
school policy, but a Board policy as well. It's not new. It's
something you're supposed to be aware of. Why did you not
fill in an incident report?"

"It wasn't completely done, but...it was partially done,"
he lied again. He knew there was no point in saying

anything else, that the best thing to do was to say as little as possible, and if possible nothing at all.

"And so?"

"So, I didn't fill out an incident report."

She made a show of closing the folder slowly, again playing the patient, kindly mentor with unpardonable irony. It was her way of mocking him.

"I know you've done most of your teaching in Bangladesh or somewhere, but you're here now. You're in Quebec. You're at Abenaki Elementary. I expect your teaching methods to reflect that. We have the Quebec Education Plan, the Reform if you want to call it that. Your task—and this is clearly spelled out—is to follow the QEP. All of us here know the great benefits of collaborative learning, and I wonder if you do? I'm surprised to see the desks in your classroom arranged in rows. The children have to sit together in groups if they're going to learn from each other. I'm surprised to hear that you read to your class. The children should be reading, not you. I'm concerned that you give your students spelling tests. You should know, as we all do, that spelling tests are of no benefit whatsoever. What matters is that the child can spell the word correctly when they use it. I'm also worried about…."

There was a knock at the door and this time he was glad of the interruption. It was the secretary with news that some parents had arrived early and had asked for him.

"Tell them he'll be right there," Maureen replied. "We're almost done."

When the door closed she stood up to indicate that the meeting was over. "We'll continue this discussion another time. This evening, don't forget to tell all your red-coded parents—those that come in—what to expect in June. And, as for Martin Thompson…"

She paused, for a ridiculously dramatic moment, just to rub salt in the wound. She had taken his entire supper hour to lecture him with lies and half truths, and now she was taking a few minutes more so that he would be late.

"I've known a great many students, first as a teacher and then as an administrator. I'm very good at reading children, and this boy has failure written all over him. If his parents come in—and they quite possibly won't because the parents of boys like this never do—I want you to be sure to warn them that their son is at risk and that next year he'll likely be at the Learning Centre. If it makes you feel better, talk about it as a possibility. That's all. You better get upstairs to your classroom. You're creating a very poor impression by not being punctual."

❧

It was twenty past nine and his last parents had just left when there was a tap at his classroom door and a woman walked in. His first impression was that she was looking for someone else. She didn't look so much a mother as a youthful grandmother. She seemed to carry a sense of energy and optimism in her step, but she had greying hair and the laugh-lines of her eyes seemed to cut deep into a face that looked strangely weathered.

"I'm sorry to come so late," she said, extending her hand which was firm and rough with calluses. "I don't want to take your time, but I did want to meet you and say thank you for everything you're doing for Martin."

"Martin?"

"I'm sorry. My name is Nicole Bonavant. My husband is Andrew Thompson. I'm Martin Thompson's mom."

"Please, have a seat." He'd arranged a few chairs in an informal circle in the little bit of space available at the front of the class. It was he who wanted to sit.

"I know Martin's a handful at school, but I am so glad that he has you as a teacher this year. You probably can't see it, but you've already made such a big difference. We've noticed a real change at home."

The puzzlement must have shown on his face.

"If I tell you a story, I think you'll understand. Martin is our youngest child, and our only boy. The spring before he turned five, we came here to enroll him for September. He was very excited about going to school. He's always been a bright child and all his sisters had always done well in school. He was looking forward so much to starting school! We got a letter at some point that spring or summer telling us that the minister of Education had made a change and, as a result, because Martin was born in October, he would not be starting Kindergarten until the following year. We told him this news but I guess we didn't check to see that he actually understood it. On the first day of school, Martin was outside, at the gate, with his sisters waiting for the school bus. He was dressed in his good clothes. He had an old bookbag and an old lunch pail which had belonged to one of the girls. I ran out just before the bus got there and I held him as we watched his sisters get on the bus and drive away. I explained to him he'd be starting school next year, and we started walking back towards the house. There's a big maple tree part way up the drive. When we got to it he swung the lunch pail as hard as he could and smashed it on the tree."

"So Martin has always hated school, and that's why he's angry? And that's why, even though he's more than capable, he won't work?"

Nicole Thompson nodded. "We had a little hope for him in Grade 2. He had a wonderful teacher. But it didn't last. That's why we were so glad when we heard you were going to be Martin's teacher. You taught Patrick Skinner two years ago."

"Yes, I remember Patrick."

"He's Martin's cousin and they're quite close. Patrick thought the world of you. You came highly recommended, and you haven't disappointed Martin in any way. You know, this is the first year that Martin has ever talked, even a little, about what he was learning in school. One day, you read something to them about an explorer, David Thompson? It was the first time that I ever saw his eyes sparkle while telling us something about school. And you know, last week, he left his spelling test on the kitchen table for us to see. He's never done anything like that before. I think he's on the verge of giving school another chance. Thank you so much. I'm sorry I came so late. We had a problem with one of the fences, which means we were late doing chores. I better let you get home. I'm sure you've had a long day. Thanks again. We really appreciate what you're doing. Please, don't change a thing. Good night. It was very nice meeting you."

As suddenly and unexpectedly as she had arrived, she was gone. He sat for a while because he didn't know what else to do, and besides, he had no energy to do more than sit. It took a very long time to actually get up and grab his empty briefcase and make it out of his room.

And now, he stood in the open doorway unable to decide on which horn he should impale himself. Before him, the icy rain, if anything, was falling even harder. Behind him the air felt unnaturally hot and stifling.

The lines of a Robert Frost poem came to him: the power of ice / is also great / and would suffice.

He hunched his thin shoulders and plunged into the storm.

My Lunch with Andrea

I don't mind at all, but I don't know if you really want to hear what I think... What I know.

It's what we lived through and it was horrible, really horrible and it left such scars, on the whole family. And sometimes I feel like such a fool that I didn't see things, or that I didn't understand them or make sense of them sooner.

I don't know where to start. It was Grade 2 that it all blew up, that I finally did something. But it started long before that. Really, where it started was at the *garderie*....

...Yes, that's right, the seven-dollar-a-day daycare...

...I know. We have a friend in the Yukon and—you probably know this—it's costing her forty-three dollars a day to put her son in daycare. In some ways we're lucky here. Now, this was six years ago and it was five-dollar-a-day daycare. And, you know, the reason we sent her to daycare wasn't that we wanted her in daycare. The last place to send your kid is to a *garderie*. God, I wish I'd acted on that! But we wanted her to have some exposure to French before starting kindergarten. We thought, it's just two days a week, she'll meet some kids; their brains are like sponges, she'll pick it up in no time. We're a unilingual family in that, at home, we live in English; although we speak French, both of us. At work it's practically all French...

...Yes, still at the same place...no, no, I do ten hours a week. It's just enough for me. I want to be home when they get off the bus. It's still important. Tommy's only in Grade 4. And God knows there's enough to do in the house ...

...No, I'm lucky. Really, I'm lucky because he does. He does a lot of the cooking and he's quite a good cook. His mother is fabulous in the kitchen—I think you met her once....

...Yes, that's right. He picked it up from her, and he enjoys it, so he does a lot of the cooking. And the kids are responsible for their own rooms, right down to the vacuuming, but there's still a lot of housework. And I also keep Jerry's books...

...I know! It's ironic but yes, I'm the bookkeeper. The first few years I did the taxes and everything. We have an accountant now. It's a business expense and it's so much easier, but I do the bookkeeping...

...Oh! I should have looked at the menu. What are you having? That sounds fine. *Oui, pour moi aussi, je prends la même chose. Oui, la salade plutôt que la soupe. Merci.* And thanks for lunch...

...Well, you're not getting much in return. Are you really sure you want to hear all this?

I was telling you about Janet... the *garderie.* It's a farce, really. You get these *bulletins* or these *comptes rendus* or whatever they call them now and what do you get? It's supposed to be an account of what your child did during the day, and it's a silly sheet of paper that says "Janet didn't eat her cheese," or some such thing and that's supposed to tell you how your child is doing!

We knew she didn't like to go. We knew that. But she went. We sent her. We knew she didn't like it but we kept thinking that these things can take a bit of time, that she's shy—and she is, she's always been a quiet child. She's an introvert—she's just like Jerry's father. And she's non-verbal, again like her grandfather. Of course, all along we kept telling ourselves that we were doing the right thing. No pain; no gain! We kept telling ourselves that even if she wasn't enthusiastic about the *garderie*, at least she was learning a bit of French. And even when we saw that she wasn't really saying much of anything in French we told ourselves that she was at least accustoming her ear… And when we dropped her off and picked her up…

You know, it wasn't until a full year later that I learned why Janet didn't want to go to daycare, and why she didn't learn a word of French. She was spending the day by herself. And I can see it. She's very happy in her own company; she can play for hours all by herself. And that's what she was doing at the *garderie*. Except that she wasn't at home where it's calm and quiet and she has practically the whole house and acres of space, she was stuck in this tight, little cranny— ok, I'm exaggerating because it's nicely painted and has lots of natural light, but it's still basically a couple of large rooms, and there is an outdoor area but it's maybe ten metres by ten metres—but it's confined compared to what she has at home. And it was full of kids and, for Janet, that just made her space smaller because she never really mixed. And this too: Tommy, who's two years younger, just among our friends, from day one, has had three great playmates who are his age. Janet, when she was two, got her brother— and they played wonderfully together, and still do—but her brother was essentially the first other child she saw. You can see, from her point of view, that the *garderie* must have been absolute purgatory for her. And it was probably worse because there was a group of three or four who were really difficult kids, aggressive kids. But we heard all this later.

And here was Janet, this quiet, introverted, non-verbal little girl of four, who, besides everything else, speaks a different language. I'm sure she spent the whole year learning only how to find a safe corner to stay out of the way.

And then she went to kindergarten and it wasn't really any different. Not that we knew it. Although there was one thing she liked in kindergarten and that was the extra French she was getting. They have a program at the school to get the kids speaking French. They do two hundred hours of intensive French...

...Yes, the child has the right to this extra period of language instruction. It's designed, really, for immigrants in bigger places like Montreal, or Sherbrooke, but if your kids come from an English home, they qualify. It's a great program, really...

...No, she got her regular classroom time, but at lunch Janet would go to see Mme Micheline and spend her lunch hour learning one-on-one...

... Well, we were very pleased because she was learning the language. And she liked it! It was the best part of her day. And we didn't question it. It wasn't until later that we figured it out. The reason she so much liked going to Mme Micheline was because it was just her with the teacher. There weren't any other kids. She was alone in this nice safe space...

...*Merci. Ça a l'air très bon.*

...No, really, not for me. If it was supper out, I'd take a glass or two, but I can't drink in the middle of the day. Not any more. But, go ahead and have one yourself...

...No. No, I can't say that. But things went along and because the signs weren't new signs we didn't see them, or we saw them without stopping to think what they meant. Janet hadn't enjoyed pre-school and, except for the two hundred hours of extra French, I don't think she liked kindergarten any better. ...

...No! Just the opposite! You know, when we finally switched her and she started at the English school, she absolutely refused to speak a single word of French. She just wouldn't do it. And she still won't. She's in Grade 6 this year and she has a wonderful teacher, who happens to be her French teacher as well, Mme Lise, and last week Janet said one sentence in French. The teacher called, just to tell me, so she's getting over it, but that's three entire years she wouldn't say a word. And it caused a few embarrassing moments for us as well. Janet's godmother is our next-door neighbour...

...Yes, Renée, you know her. Well, Renée, as you know, is a unilingual francophone. And they're our next-door neighbours and we don't necessarily see them every day, but we do see them, and they do come over for supper, as we go over there for supper. It was awkward, but I understood and we tried to encourage her, but at the same time we didn't want to force her, you know, "Speak French to Renée or you go to your room," you know what I mean? And I know Renée understood as well, but just the same. I understand it, because Janet felt hurt and she had to get rid of that hurt, but getting rid of it ended up hurting her godmother, and us too...

...No, it wasn't. No, Tommy's experience was completely different. But he's such a different child. And, as well, his circumstances weren't at all the same. The biggest thing, I think, was that when he started kindergarten, there were three other English boys in the group, two of them boys he's been friends with practically since he was born. Janet was all alone, both emotionally and linguistically speaking. She didn't know anyone. She didn't speak, let alone speak

French. And she's not a child who makes friends quickly. Tommy's so easy-going and he's got this little disarming smile and that wins everybody over in half a second. He makes friends, regardless of language, and as I said, he had a natural support group. I hadn't really thought of this before, but when he started at the English school, it was the same thing, he had friends there from day one.

But even with Tommy, when he started school, at the French school, there was a big change in him. We didn't see it so much at home, in fact, we didn't see it at all, but at school, almost from the very beginning, he was always getting into scraps. By nature, Tommy's not like that. He has his father's temperament. He really is an easy-going child, always has been. When he was just little, a two-year old in the sandbox, I remember this so clearly, when it happened I was almost worried that there was something wrong with him. He was in the sandbox with Michael, I think you might remember Sandra Corris? The two boys are virtually the same age. Tommy had some toy in his hand, and Michael reached over to grab it. The natural thing to expect is that Tommy would hold onto the toy even harder and cling to it. It was his toy. He was playing with it. But, no. He gave the little shovel, or whatever it was to Michael and smiled at him. It was so unreal. But he's like that. He's generous and caring.

Anyway, Michael was one of the boys with him, and Paul Théroux is the other one. They were all three together plus another little English boy, the son of the Anglican minister. And I know them. They're not aggressive little boys in any way. They're not! We know them all. We see them often. If a kid is aggressive, if he has issues, if there's a problem, you see it. And there had never been a problem. Never. Yet, a month after they started school, all four of them were constantly getting into little scraps of some kind or another in the playground. And you know, it didn't ever completely stop...

Oui, merci. C'était excellent. Très bon....

...No, we transferred him over to the English school last year. He started Grade 3 in English...

...No. He was doing well. And he never complained really. No, we transferred him because it was just easier to have the two kids in the same school system. You don't have to worry about juggling two different school calendars. They're both off school on the same days. They catch the same bus at the same time. There are half as many parents' nights. But you know, we're glad we did move him. He's happier.

Because there were things going on with Tommy too. He never said a word. He never complained the way Janet did, but you know, after he started at the English school, every night, for I don't know how many months, every night he woke us up with nightmares and they were always about school. Not the new school he was attending, but the old school.

And it struck us as so strange because...

...*Merci. C'est une belle assiette. Non, c'est beau. Peut-être juste un peu d'eau. Merci...*

...Yes, isn't it?

...No, they've been open a couple of years I think. There was a great place in town here several years ago. I don't know if you ever got a chance to eat there. It was called *L'Abbé qui rit.* Yes. Strange name but it was a clever play on words. A bilingual play on words. It had started as a bakery. The place had great bread and incredible desserts...

...Yes, Janet. I'm sorry. I know I'm all over the place. Grade 2. But, before I tell you about Grade 2, I want you to understand that we really did try to stay involved in our kids' education. We always read to the kids, Jerry as well. Especially when they were small, Jerry used to make up bedtime stories for them. And we had all sorts of children's books and we'd read them to sleep—though it also happened that we'd read ourselves to sleep. All of a sudden, you've got this little three- or four-year-old tugging on your arm, upset with you because you've fallen asleep in the middle of a sentence. But you know, they were both reading before they started school. They just learned. They loved to hear the same stories over and over and at a certain point they just start following word for word what you're reading and the next thing you know your child can read. It's remarkable, really.

So we were involved. And we tried to get involved in the school as well. I was a library volunteer, which meant that twice a month I'd go into the school to shelve books and tidy up the furniture or maybe make a poster for a special event. And when they had field trips and they needed *des parents accompagnateurs*, I was almost always the first to volunteer. I still do. Jerry has also gone on day trips, but it's harder for him. And I want to tell you this too, the year Janet was in Grade 1—and by this time we knew there was something wrong, even if we hadn't yet put our finger on it—but when she was in Grade 1, I had this idea that it might be helpful if a couple of parents—and there were a few others who were interested in doing this with me—to get a couple of parents who would organize some non-competitive games that the kids could play during the noon hour. Because they have a long stretch at noon. The kids eat in about two minutes flat and then they're outside on the playground for over an hour. Anyway, we spoke to the noon-hour supervisors and they thought it was a great idea and they were all for it. But when I proposed it to Janet's teacher, she said they'd have to talk about it at the *Conseil d'école*. For whatever reason, it had to go through one committee and then another and had to be approved here, there, and everywhere and to make a long story short, months after we'd proposed this it all came to nothing.

It wasn't a big thing, but I remember feeling really down about it. It was a moment of really deep, profound disillusionment. It was discovering you're being lied to, that you're told one thing—that your involvement as a parent is important to your child's success—you should see the pamphlets and the literature they send home. But really, the truth is, the school does not want you because you're a parent and like Victorian children, parents are meant to be seen—on particular occasions like parents' night—but not heard. Nobody really wants to hear what a parent might have to say.

And the other thing about Janet going into Grade 2 was that, more and more, she'd been complaining about school. It had started at some point in Grade 1 that she'd say, "Do I have to go to school today?" or "I don't want to go to school today," and along with that, she started complaining of pain in her back, between her shoulder blades and into her neck. At first we'd say did you fall, or did you bang into something, or did someone hit you? Not that there was anything to see, but she complained more and more and eventually we brought her to the doctor and of course there wasn't anything that he could see either.

I can't remember now how long this went on. Well, most of Grade 2 because it all came to a head in the spring, at the end of April. But it was an awful year. For one thing, the school got a new principal, a new *directeur* and he was a disaster—for everyone. By the end of the year there were so many complaints—from the teachers—that they moved him to Adult Ed. But he was completely wrong in every way imaginable. He had no experience with small children. He had been a high school vice principal, and any teaching experience he had was at the high school level. On top of that, he had no knowledge of this area. I don't know what cesspit they dredged up to find him. I mean, it was as if he'd never seen a single immigrant, or heard a word of English before coming here. And, yes, it's a French school, and yes, French is the official language, but there's still a sizable English community here and there are lots of English families that choose to send their kids to French school because they think that's the best way to make their kids perfectly bilingual...

...Exactly, just like us. Anyway there was this new *directeur*, and he was all wrong. He was an awful man. He was big, shoulders out to here, shaved head. He looked like one of those big, stupid football players or something. He knew his size was intimidating and he played it up, the way he walked, swaggering with his shoulders ready to knock down anything in his way. His teachers hated him. What we heard was that he was moved because practically every teacher in the school had filed an official grievance of some sort against him. At least they moved him to Adult Ed and not another elementary school. Probably do less harm there, although it makes you wonder what someone like that is doing in a school in the first place. He just didn't belong in an elementary school. But that seems to be the way it is now, they just move them around every couple of years...

...It's like bank managers. There are exceptions, but generally speaking, bank managers get moved around every few years. The bank wants the manager's undivided loyalty. Someone who stays in the same place too long just might develop some kind of allegiance to the community and maybe act in some way which is primarily beneficial to a client rather than the bank. School principals get shuffled around the same way, and for the same reason. I've heard the same thing is starting to happen with teachers. The young ones in particular, it seems, do a year or two in one school and then get shipped off somewhere else…

…Yes, I'm sorry, I'm always going off on tangents. What I was telling you was that there was this new *directeur*, and from the very first time I talked to him it was confrontational. I think with him it was all about power or ego or something. It had nothing to do with the kids…

…No, it was about Tommy. And it was innocent enough. I mean, I wasn't trying to be a pushy parent or anything. But Tommy had started kindergarten and, like his sister, he was eligible for this intensive language program. And, in his case, there were four little boys who were supposed to be getting the extra French…

…Yes, exactly. A week rolled by, a month rolled by and Tommy still hadn't started the extra French. In Janet's case, she had started I think the first or second day of school and I couldn't understand why it was taking so long for Tommy to start. I contacted Mme Sylvie, Tommy's teacher, and she didn't know, but she suggested I talk to the *directeur*.…

…No! No, it's just the way they do it on the French side, all the teachers, everyone, is called by his or her first name. It's got to be a cultural thing. And, it's funny, at the English school it's Mr. Jones and Ms Smith, but the French teacher is Mme Christine, or Mme Suzanne or whatever the first name is…

…Yes, so I call. I call to ask when these little boys would be starting their two hundred hours of French and he says to me, *"Je ne sais pas de quoi vous parlez, Madame,"* and it wasn't the words—although those are bad enough—but the tone in his voice. Utterly dismissive. I started to explain the program and that Janet had followed it and, just like that, he cut me off, *"Je vais me renseigner,"* and he hung up on me. No "goodbye," no "I'll call you back," nothing. He just threw down the receiver.

But nothing happened. Every day I'd ask Tommy. We waited one week, two weeks. I called the other parents and everybody was a little concerned but nobody wanted to phone him. At this point, at least three weeks had gone by, so I call the school again. And again on the phone, I can almost feel this antagonism. *"Oui, Madame. Les arrangements nécessaires ont été pris."* Click! That's it. But when we asked Tommy if he had started doing his extra French at noon, he said no. We call Mme Sylvie and she doesn't know any more than we do. I call the other parents, the other three English parents, and this time Linda agrees to come with me to meet the *directeur*.

We phone the school to ask for a meeting and I wait five minutes, but finally the secretary comes back to the phone and tells me that he will see us at two in the afternoon. Linda's as concerned as I am and we're there at five to two. We wait and we wait and finally I tell the secretary that we had a meeting with the *directeur* at two o'clock. She comes back two minutes later and tells us that he's busy for at least another half hour or more but that we could wait.

No, I said, that was fine. We'd go for a walk and come back in half an hour. I wasn't going to sit outside the principal's office like some truant ten year-old. And we knew he was just playing games with us. He didn't want to see us and this was his way of getting rid of us. We didn't go more than twenty steps from the front door and the secretary was calling us back.

He was seeing us only because he knew we weren't going to go away but he wasn't any more pleasant with the two of us than he had been with me on the phone. *"Quelqu'un a été engagé,"* he said but when we asked why our kids hadn't yet started the program, he went off on a long tangent about classrooms and schedules and all sorts of things that were coming out of left field. Finally, I asked him when the kids would be starting their intensive French. *"Bientôt,"* he said, *"maintenant, je suis très occupé."* He jumped up behind his desk and that was the end of the meeting. It was ridiculous.

But the next day, Tommy finally started doing the noon-hour French...

You can't imagine sometimes how inadequate I feel that I don't have a university degree...

...Yes, I know...

...That's true...

...No, I am. But still, sometimes...

...Yes, Janet! While all this was going on with Tommy, things with Janet weren't going any better. What we didn't realize—and we should have—was that the same small group of kids who had been in Janet's *garderie* were just following her up through the successive grades. The same kids who had made the *garderie* such a negative experience were still there in the same class. And Janet was coming home and complaining of these pains, and not wanting to go to school and...

...Oh, no! No, girls don't hit. It's not physical with girls. No, it's all psychological, emotional. It's "I'm not going to be your friend." It's ostracism. At one point, a little girl said to Janet, "I'd like to be your friend, but I can't because if I'm friends with you they said I can't be friends with them." And she turned her back and walked away.

You know, when Tommy started at the English school, one of his friends—well, Andy, you know, Mary's oldest—he pulled him aside on the first day of school and pointed out all the kids on the playground. Watch out for him because he punches, and be careful with her because she steals. And you know—the teachers would be surprised because they all think that she's a little princess—but the worst bully in the school was a girl in Grade 6. Andy told Tommy, stay away from her and don't let her come near you. She's big trouble.

But we didn't know. The irony is that now the big thing in schools is socializing the child—learning math or language is almost like a little side dish, the real aim is socialization—but all Janet was feeling was complete isolation. Her teacher was this woman, Mme Jacqueline, who's the exact opposite of anything we would ever have wanted in a teacher. Maybe I'm being unfair, but she was like a Barbie. Hair out to here. Dressed like she was stepping off a fashion runway. I didn't see this woman every single day but I did see her a lot and I don't think I ever saw her wearing the same outfit twice. Nails painted to match her eye makeup, loaded down with costume jewelry...

...You laugh, but I'm not kidding. If you met her somewhere the last thing you would imagine this lady does to earn a living is teach a Grade 2 class. If I never see her again, it'll be too soon.

And she was a screamer...

...A screamer is what they call a teacher who screams when she gets upset with a child...

...Ha! Yes, you're right. But you can see that the last thing Janet needed was a screamer. It wouldn't matter that Mme Jacqueline was screaming at the kid beside her, or even at some kid at the other end of the classroom, Janet would be the one traumatized by it. She's a sensitive kid, maybe a little too sensitive... So it was all wrong for her and we didn't see it, or didn't want to see it maybe.

And I'm to blame too because I was there. That's the most amazing thing. I was there. Every second Tuesday morning, I was doing my turn in the library. I would walk down those corridors, and I would see those people: the kids and the teachers and the janitor and the secretary. I think I was trying really hard to project all my good intentions onto the place. I think that's why I didn't see it. It was what we wanted for her. To be fluent in both languages. And it did just the opposite.

But it must have been awful for her in that school. The last two or three times I was in that building, it almost literally made my skin crawl. And it must have been like that for her every single day.

And you know, I kept asking Mme Jacqueline. Every time I went in, I always tried to see her just for a minute, just to ask. And it went from *Comment ça va avec Janet ?* to *Qu'est-ce qu'il y a qui ne va pas avec Janet ? Pourquoi est-ce qu'elle n'aime pas l'école ?* I knew there was something wrong. We knew. Every single morning she'd have these pains and she'd be crying and asking to stay home. But every time I talked to Mme Jacqueline, we might start talking about Janet, but it always went off on a tangent and she'd end up talking about her own problems: she had too many kids in the class; she didn't have enough books; she had to accommodate a student on crutches; her photocopying budget had been slashed. And then, the second-last time I saw her, she went off on her usual tangent but this time, she started telling me what a hard year it was, how she had a half a dozen coded students—*des cas de comportement graves*—and I went home just as frustrated with her, but somehow with a bell ringing in my head.

I'd just come from there, but I phoned the school and made an appointment with the *directeur*, for the very next day. And it was so frustrating, so humiliating almost. I went in and tried telling him there was something wrong. *"Il y a quelque chose qui ne va pas,"* I told him. And I told him yes, I'd spoken to Mme Jacqueline, who knows how many times, and I told him about the pain in the shoulders and neck that Janet was complaining about, and the way she cried in the morning not to go to school. And he sat there and looked at me the way he might look at an insect with two heads. I can't describe it to you, but there was something about his face, his eyes, his posture, that told me he couldn't care less. *"Je suis très préoccupée,"* I told him. He said he'd look into it and stood up to let me know the meeting was over and I didn't know what to do. I felt like crying but I'd be damned if I was going to cry in front of him. I just sat there stewing, feeling so angry that I couldn't talk to him, that he wouldn't listen, that he didn't care.

I finally left. I don't think I even said goodbye. I certainly didn't say thank you, although I knew that was also a mistake. I know when I got into the car, I sat there for I don't know how long with tears streaming down my face but I wasn't crying. It was just tears.

I wasn't home five minutes when the phone rang and it was the school asking me if I could come and pick Janet up, that something was wrong.

I rush back to the school, I rush up the stairs to her classroom and what do I see? Janet is laid out on the floor with a blanket over her, up to her chin. Her eyes are shut tight, not in sleep, because you can she she's forcing them shut tight. Mme Jacqueline is kneeling beside her, playing nurse, fanning her face. *Qu'est-ce qui s'est passé ?* I ask her and even as I'm asking Janet the same question in English,

Mme Jacqueline answers, *Elle s'est écroulée et elle a du mal à se relever.* And then, without so much as a pause between sentences, she says, *Janet et moi, on pense que Janet serait plus heureuse à l'école anglaise...*

I could have collapsed, like Janet, stretched out on the floor. Or I could just as easily have scratched her eyes out, if I had nails like hers. My daughter is stretched out on the floor unable to get up and you pick this moment to discuss choosing the right school? I have come to see you dozens of times to ask you why my daughter is so unhappy in school and you tell me absolutely nothing, on the contrary, you keep assuring me that everything's fine and now my daughter collapses on the floor and you tell me she should change school? That's the solution to a problem that, so far, you have told me doesn't even exist?

I was livid. I think I looked at her for a minute but I didn't say a word to her.

No, I did. I said *Laisse-la.* The big hair gave me a look but she backed away.

I looked at Janet and it was so strange. It was like an out-of-body experience. It was as if I was somewhere else, a spectator watching my own body as it moved through this unreal event. I leaned over Janet for a second and spoke to her. I've come to bring you home, I said. Or something like that. I know I was perfectly calm and I also knew—and don't ask me how—but I knew what had happened and what to do. I spoke to her again. We're going home now, I told her. And I kept speaking. I spoke softly and calmly as if what had happened, what was happening, was as natural and harmless as snow falling in January. I understood that Janet's body had somehow seized. She was frozen. What she had been experiencing in her shoulders and neck had taken hold of her entire body. All I wanted to do was get her out of there. Somehow, between talking to her and lifting her, I managed to get her upright and moving. It was as if, instead of being flesh and bones, as if she was made of metal and all her joints had rusted up. Like the Tin Man. It was very slow and for her, I know, it was painful.

And as we were slowly hobbling down the stairs, with me half supporting Janet who could hardly move, the *directeur* passed us on the stairs. He went by us as if we weren't there. Ignored us totally. I can't tell you how small that made me feel, how that hurt. Here was this man—and big muscles and all, I don't think he's a man; he's the very opposite of what a man should be—so here's this individual who, as the one in charge of the well-being of the couple of hundred students in that building, should be the first to pause at least long enough to say, hello Janet, I hope you'll be better tomorrow. And if he wasn't so busy doing nothing, he might even have asked what was wrong and seen if he could help. And did he not see I was the same person who had been in his office not even an hour earlier expressing concern about my child who now seemed to be half crippled? And he climbed right by!

It was awful. I know it sounds ridiculous now that I talk about it. So what if he walked by without saying hello? How many people walk by me without saying hello? I know it sounds silly, but in that instant, the way he pretended we didn't exist hurt me as much as if he'd picked me up and thrown me down the stairs....

...Yes, that's true. That's very true. I've seen it with my own eyes. Let me tell you this one little story. This was a couple of years ago. It was one of the kids' birthday parties. We've always made the birthdays a shared celebration, both Janet and Tommy invite friends over. Anyway, one of Tommy's little friends, a very active little boy by the name of Steven

Robert—and he's francophone, even if his name is Steven— he was playing near my flower beds—where he knew he wasn't supposed to be—and he took a terrible tumble. He was up by the rock garden and somehow he fell. I saw it happen. I swear I thought we'd be bringing him to the Emergency with broken bones. You wouldn't believe the tumble he took. But he bounced right up and looked puzzled for a second but went right on as if nothing had happened.

Well, that same little boy, ten minutes later was in tears because he wanted a different coloured party hat and his sister—his little sister—wouldn't trade with him. No, what you asked earlier, if there was anything physical? From what I've seen, I'd say kids handle and recover from physical trauma so much more easily than emotional or psychological attacks...

...*Oh! Je prends cette dernière petite bouchée. C'était très bon, merci. Les légumes étaient cuits à la perfection. Très bon...*

...Well, I've already eaten more than I normally do at lunch, but if you're having some I'll join you...

...*Non, je vais essayer la crème caramel. Oui, merci. Oh, oui, pourquoi pas, je prends un café aussi. Merci.*

...There was something I read recently, or that I heard somewhere, and it really struck me. It was about human needs, a list of what we need to survive. It was a short list, four or five things, and I can't remember now exactly, but we need food and we need shelter but we also need the emotional support of others... And I think that's why it hurt so much when he marched right by us on that staircase. He was announcing in no uncertain terms that we would be getting no emotional support from him...

A principal makes such a difference to a school...

...*Merci! Ça a l'air délicieux!* Yours looks good too.

...Yes, principals and the difference they make. A good principal really does make a difference. It's the principal who sets the tone, who gives the school its essential culture. Really. It was night and day for Janet...

...No, no, the following September...

...I sent her to my Mom's place. I certainly wasn't sending her back to that school. She went to her granny's, and she was perfectly fine. There was not a thing wrong with her. Her shoulders didn't hurt and her neck didn't hurt and she was a perfectly happy and contented little girl. She got a four-month summer holiday, most of it at her granny's.

In September, she started at the English school and I think she was a little apprehensive. I certainly was. But you know, the first day, I drove her and we stayed in the car for a minute and watched some of the kids getting off the buses and when she was ready we got out of the car and started walking to the part of the yard where the kids line up and there, all of a sudden, was Lee Fitzpatrick, the principal, and she greeted Janet and told her she hoped she'd like her new school and to go and see her any time she wanted to about anything at all. And she looked at Janet as she spoke to her and I can't say enough good about her. She's wonderful for that school and I just pray they won't shuffle her off somewhere else before Tommy finishes...

...*Merci! C'était vraiment très bon... Non, merci, une tasse c'est assez... Non, rien d'autre pour moi...*

...I don't know if you've looked at your watch but it's almost two...

...No, I'm ok. I'll pick up the kids, since I'm in town, but they don't finish till 3:15. I've got lots of time. It's more for you...

...It was great to see you too. And thanks for lunch. You didn't have to...

...No, absolutely not. Everything I told you, I'd be happy to repeat in a court of law...

...It is awful. And I'm serious when I say that it leaves scars. And it's not just kids it happens to. You know, there's someone you really should meet. The next time you come down, if all this stuff is still interesting to you, I'll bring you to meet Marcel St-Amand. He's a neighbour of ours, over on the Fourth Rang. A very nice man, probably close to sixty now. He was a teacher—and if you talk to him for two minutes, you'll see right away that he must have been a very good teacher. He suffered a burnout and took an early retirement. This was several years ago. Now he does biodynamic gardening—and you should see his place. But the reason you should speak to him is because you'd find his stories very interesting, or I should say, very disturbing. Now here's the kicker: what he went through still affects him to the point that he's seeing a therapist...

...I can do that. I'll talk to him and I'll put you in touch. I'm sure he'd be glad to talk to you. He's very articulate and if you have any gardening questions, he's a walking Wikipedia...

...No, that won't be a problem. He speaks English quite well. And you must still have some French, even if it's rusty...

...I will. Yes. And you never know, we might just surprise you one day and show up on your doorstep, four of us plus the dog...

...We've actually been talking about it. Janet's in high school next year. God, and isn't that another worry! But we've been talking about taking some time to travel before the kids are all grown...

...I know you've got to be going...

...Let me at least get the tip.

Acknowledgements

Principals and Other Schoolyard Bullies is a work of fiction and the stories in the book are very much a creation of my own imagination. Still, my imagination was at times inspired by random comments, by brief anecdotes but also by very serious events which, sadly, were all too real. I am grateful to a number of people who, while they still carry the emotional scars of their experiences, were nevertheless willing to share their stories with me and consented to have them fictionalized. I am equally grateful to friends and family who read my text and brought to it many more corrections and improvements than I would feel comfortable to divulge.

I first wish to thank Robin Philpot for once again undertaking all the risks involved in publishing a book during these demanding economic times. I must also thank Denis Palmer, whose deft skill with pen and ink I can only envy. Others to whom I am indebted include: Muriel Allen, Francine Beaubien, Ron Booth, Barry Evans, Karine Fonda, David Fonda, Royce Griffith, Sharon and Ralph McCully, Julie Miller, Eric St-Louis, Ronald Tardif, and Zoe Whittall.

Nick FONDA, Richmond, Quebec, August, 2011

AVAILABLE OR FORTHCOMING FROM BARAKA BOOKS
www.barakabooks.com

FICTION AND CREATIVE NONFICTION

Roads to Richmond: Portraits of Quebec's Eastern Townships by Nick Fonda

Break Away: Jessie on my mind by Sylvain Hotte

You could lose an eye, My first 80 years in Montreal by David Reich

I Hate Hockey by François Barcelo (October 2011)

HISTORY AND POLITICAL ISSUES

Barack Obama and the Jim Crow Media, The return of the nigger breakers
Ishmael Reed

A People's History of Quebec
Jacques Lacoursière & Robin Philpot

*America's Gift, What the world owes to the Americas
and their first inhabitants*
Käthe Roth and Denis Vaugeois

The Question of Separatism, Quebec and the Struggle over Sovereignty
Jane Jacobs

An Independent Quebec, The past, the present and the future
Jacques Parizeau

Joseph-Elzéar Bernier, Champion of Canadian Arctic Sovereignty
Marjolaine Saint-Pierre

Trudeau's Darkest Hour, War Measures in time of peace, October 1970
Edited by Guy Bouthillier & Édouard Cloutier

*The Riot that Never Was
The military shooting of three Montrealers in 1832 and the official cover-up*
James Jackson

Discrimination in the NHL, Quebec Hockey Players Sidelined
Bob Sirois

Printed in Canada
on Enviro 100% recycled
at Lebonfon Printing.